# MY FRIEND WALTER

***Also by Michael Morpurgo***

Arthur: High King of Britain
Escape From Shangri-La
Friend or Foe
The Ghost of Grania O'Malley
Kensuke's Kingdom
King of the Cloud Forests
Little Foxes
Long Way Home
Mr Nobody's Eyes
Twist of Gold
Waiting for Anya
War Horse
The War of Jenkins' Ear
The White Horse of Zennor
Why the Whales Came

***For younger readers***

Conker
The Marble Crusher
The Nine Lives of Montezuma
The Sandman and the Turtles

***Edited by Michael Morpurgo***

Muck and Magic: Stories from the Countryside
More Muck and Magic

# MY FRIEND WALTER

## MICHAEL MORPURGO

**CHILDREN'S LAUREATE**

EGMONT

*For Christine and Dave,*
*Zoé and Orlanda,*
*Fredi and Lotta*

First published in Great Britain in 1988
by William Heinemann Ltd
Reissued 2001 by Egmont Books Ltd
239 Kensington High Street, London W8 6SA



ISBN 0 7497 4671 8

8 10 9

A CIP catalogue record for this title is available from the British Library

Printed and bound in Great Britain by Cox & Wyman Ltd, Reading, Berkshire

# CHAPTER 1

BEFORE I TELL YOU ABOUT THE POSTCARD I HAD better tell you something about me. My name is Elizabeth Throckmorton and I'll be eleven on my next birthday. Aunty Ellie (you'll meet her later) calls me her 'china doll' on account of my pale skin and straight black hair. I'm small for my age, so people at school think I'm feeble and fragile which I'm not. I don't talk much, so they think I'm unfriendly which I'm not. I just get on better with myself than anyone else, that's all.

Around me at home there's my family. First there's Father, who's a farmer. Father treats me like a boy. I think he always wanted me to be a boy, really. Then there's Mother, who's always busy. If she's not out on the farm she's scurrying about the house with a broom or a pile of dirty washing. She never stops. She doesn't seem to have time to talk to me much these days, not since Little Jim was born; but we understand each other – always have done. Not like my big brother Will. We haven't got much in common, Will and me. When he's not shooting or fishing, he's down in the cellar making horrible smells in the chemistry laboratory he's set up down there. I'd like to like him more – I know I ought to.

Then there's Little Jim. Little Jim was born about eight months ago. He always needs feeding or changing or picking up or mopping up. I spend a lot of time looking after Little Jim, but he doesn't seem to appreciate it. He loves to pull my hair out by the roots or to tear my ears off whenever he can. He never does that to Gran. Gran has been living with us in the house for as long as I can remember. She's nearly eighty now. I know she means well, but she does go on a bit sometimes.

I suppose you could say that it was an ordinary sort of a morning in our house the day the postcard came. The toast burnt and Father shouted and spluttered with his mouth full of cornflakes. I was giving Little Jim his breakfast. Mother was trying to rescue the toast and to see to Gran's boiled egg, all at the same time. Will was in the bathroom. He's always down last. Humph is our black and white sheepdog with a killer instinct for letters and postcards, and it was Humph that heard the postman first. He rose with a terrible growl from his catching position under Little Jim's high chair and fairly flew out of the kitchen door. He returned seconds later, his tail high with triumph, a postcard in his mouth, wet and punctured as usual. Mother told him to drop it. Humph looked at her blankly, pretending not to understand. He had learned that if you hold out long enough you get one of Little Jim's rusks in exchange for the post. And sure enough he got one this morning.

'Well, I'm blowed,' Father said, picking the postcard off the floor. 'What do you make of this, then?'

'Of what, dear?' said Mother, wiping her hands on her apron and coming to look over his shoulder.

'Can't hardly make it out,' said Father, peering at it closely. ''S funny writing, don't you think? Anyway, seems we're all invited to some sort of family reunion. Never heard of such a thing, have you?'

'What's it say?' I asked, looking at the picture on the back of the postcard. It was of the Tower of London with a Beefeater standing outside looking very serious.

'It says: "To the family Throckmorton" – that means you too, Jimmy.' Little Jim waved his arms up and down like a tin drummer boy and then rubbed his soggy rusk in his ear. 'It says: "You are invited to attend a grand reunion of our family to be held at the Tower Hotel, London, on the fourteenth of July at noon. Have your name writ upon you so we may know one another".'

'Very mysterious,' said Mother. 'I wonder who sent it. Can't spell, whoever it is. Should be "written" not "writ".

And it's not signed at all. Just look at the writing, Bess. Worse than yours.' And she turned the card round to show me. The handwriting was all squeezed up and tall. I could hardly read a word of it.

'Rum business if you ask me,' said Father. 'Could be a hoax for all we know.'

'Nonsense,' Mother said. 'People have family reunions all the time. I think it's a lovely idea. I'd love to go, but the fourteenth – I think something's happening on the fourteenth.' And she went over to look at the calendar by the phone. 'Oh dear, I thought so. We can't go, not on the fourteenth. You've got to see the accountant in the afternoon, dear. Little Jim's got his diphtheria jab in the morning at the doctor's. And you were coming with us, Gran, for your check-up, remember? What a pity.' Gran was about to protest. 'It would be too much for you anyway, Gran. You know what the doctor said about overdoing it. And Will's still away at camp with the school. Where did they say they're having it?'

'The Tower Hotel, it says here,' said Father. 'Up in London. Somewhere near the Tower of London, I suppose.'

'That's where they cut off all those heads,' said my brother Will, doing up his trousers as he came in the door. He growled at Humph as usual, who growled back as usual. 'I've been there,' said Will. 'I've seen the very place where they cut off their heads. I've seen the axe. Sharp as a razor it was. Mind you, one of them Beefeaters said it sometimes needed three or four swipes if your neck was a bit thick.'

'Will!' said Mother. 'That's quite enough. Now sit down and eat your breakfast.' She turned to me. 'But you can go, Bessy. If we could find someone to take you, you could go.' I shook my head. I didn't like parties at all and there'd be lots of strange people. 'Bound to be lots of other children there,' Mother went on. 'You'd like to meet your cousins, wouldn't you? I wonder if Aunty Ellie got an invitation. She'd take you, I know she would.'

The telephone rang, and Mother was right beside it. It was Aunty Ellie; and yes, she'd had an invitation. No, hers wasn't signed either, and yes, she'd take along anyone who wanted to go. Everyone told me I should go. 'Nothing ventured, nothing gained,' said Gran. 'Be interesting,' said Mother. So I went.

As it turned out the party wasn't a bit interesting, not to start with, anyway. Once at the hotel, I trailed around after Aunty Ellie through a sea of relations that I had never met who peered at the name on my label – as the invitation had said, everyone wore labels so we could find out who we all were – and they asked me where I lived and where the rest of my family was and where I went to school and what hobbies I had. I would tell them I liked reading books and painting pictures and following butterflies – for some reason that seemed to make them laugh. I can't think why. I ate two flakey sausage rolls which were delicious, some apple tart which was not, and drank glasses of orange juice. I glared back at a few distant cousins who glared at me, and then because my legs were tired and because I couldn't really cope with my third sausage roll and a sticky bun and an orange juice all at the same time, I looked for somewhere to sit down.

I left Aunty Ellie chatting to an aged great uncle who wore striped braces to hold his trousers up over his huge stomach, and went to sit by myself on an empty sofa. Everyone seemed to have a lot to say to everyone and there must have been some good jokes (although I didn't hear any) because they were all laughing a lot and loudly. I had finished my sausage roll and was wondering which end of my sticky bun to bite into when I noticed there was someone else sitting beside me. It startled me because I'd thought until that moment that I was alone.

Sitting on the far end of the sofa was an old man with a silver-topped cane. He was swathed in a long black cloak which covered him from head to toe. He was smoking a pipe, a long elegant silver pipe; and he was leaning forward over the top of his cane studying my label and then my face. 'So you are Elizabeth Throckmorton?'

I nodded.

'I have been searching for you.' He looked at me more closely and smiled and shook his head. 'Long ago I knew someone of the same name,' he said. 'She was older, I grant you, yet the likeness is unquestionable. You have her eyes, you have her face.' His voice was strangely reedy and high-pitched, and he spoke with a burr much as we do in Devon. He seemed to be waiting for me to say something, but it was hard to know what to say, and so I said nothing. The old man began to chuckle as he looked around the room. 'If Sir Walter himself could be here,' he said, 'I wonder indeed what he would think of his family.'

'Sir Walter?'

'Sir Walter Raleigh!' he said rather sternly. 'You have heard of him I trust?'

'Yes, I think so,' I said. 'Wasn't he the one that laid his cloak in a puddle so Queen Elizabeth could walk across without getting her feet wet?'

The old man looked at me long and hard and then sat back on the sofa and shook his head sadly. 'Is that all you know about Sir Walter Raleigh? Well, you should know more. Do you not know that he is an ancestor of yours?'

'Of mine?'

'A distant relative I grant you, but everyone in this room has the blood of Walter Raleigh running in their veins, albeit thinly.' He drew on his pipe and sighed as he looked around him. 'It is hard to believe it, but it is so.' He turned to me again. 'He lived close by for some time, you know.'

'Close by?' I said.

'In the Tower of London. If ever a man served his country

well it was Walter Raleigh – and how did they repay him? They locked him up and cut off his head.'

'Cut off his head? But why?'

'That is indeed a long story and a hard one for me to tell.' He leaned forward again and spoke gently. 'But since you have some connection with him by blood, perhaps you should go and see where he lived all those years ago. Thirteen years he was there. Thirteen long, cold years in the Bloody Tower. You should go there child. You should see it.' He gripped my arm so tightly that it frightened me, and looked at me earnestly. 'He is part of your history. He is part of you. Will you go?'

'I'll try,' I said, and he seemed happy with that.

He looked past me. 'I long for something to drink, child; but there is a crush of people about the table.'

'I'll fetch it,' I said. 'Tea?'

He smiled at me. 'Wine,' he replied. 'Red wine. I drink nothing else. I shall be here or hereabouts when you return.' When he stood up he was a lot taller than I expected. I looked up into his face. His beard was white and pointed, and he seemed for a moment unsteady on his feet. 'Back in a minute,' I said.

I suppose I was gone a little longer than that because there was a queue for the wine, but when I came back he was nowhere to be seen. I asked after him everywhere but no one seemed to have noticed a tall old man in a black cloak carrying a silver-topped cane. I thought I had found him once and tugged at a black-cloaked figure talking to Aunty Ellie, but he turned out to be a vicar in his cape and so I offered him the wine anyway to cover my embarrassment. Aunty Ellie was delighted at my politeness. She introduced me as her little niece, her 'little china doll'; and I was once more yoked to her skirts and paraded around amongst my inquisitive relatives. But I remember little enough of the party after that for all I could think of was the tall old man who had appeared and then disappeared, who had insisted that I visit the Tower where Walter Raleigh had been locked up all those years. The more I thought about it, the more I wanted to go; but I wondered how on earth I was going to persuade Aunty Ellie to take me.

In the end, though, it was Aunty Ellie herself who suggested it. She had met up with a long-lost cousin of hers whom she had not seen since she was a child and I suppose they wanted something to keep me happy, or quiet, whilst they reminisced about the childhood summer holidays they had spent together by the sea at somewhere called Whitstable. We could either go on a trip up the river or to the Tower, Aunty Ellie said. Which did I want? 'The Tower,' I said. And so I found myself that afternoon inside the Tower of London walking past red-coated, bearskinned guards whose eyes wouldn't even move when I looked up into them, past Beefeaters who smiled down at me and curled their abundant moustaches as if they were Father Christmases.

As we stood in the queue waiting to see the Crown Jewels, I tried to ask Aunty Ellie about Walter Raleigh. After all, if he was related to me he was related to her too. She told me not to interrupt and finished telling her blue-haired cousin, Miss Soper I was to call her, all about her life as a midwife, about how she had looked after almost all the new-born babies born in Devon for over thirty years and how so many of them were named after her. 'Now dear,' she said, turning to me at last, 'what was it?'

'Someone at the party told me we were related to Walter Raleigh.' Aunty Ellie opened her mouth to speak, but Miss Soper got there first.

'Indeed, we are, dear,' said Miss Soper. 'But thankfully only distantly, and on his wife's side. He was a terrible rogue, that one. He was imprisoned here, you know.'

'I know,' I said.

'And he was a traitor,' said Miss Soper. 'That's why he had his head chopped off. We are much more proud of our Sir Francis Drake connection, aren't we Ellie? The Sopers are related much more directly to the Drakes than the Raleighs. Now there was a man if there ever was one. Francis Drake.' She took a deep breath. 'Drake is in his hammock and a thousand miles away . . .' and Miss Soper began to recite a poem in such a loud and impassioned way that the whole queue gathered around her to listen, and then clapped when she had finished. 'I think, Ellie,' she said, giggling with embarrassment, 'I think I drank a teeny weeny bit too much wine at the party.'

'I think so too,' said Aunty Ellie, 'But what does it matter? Oh, it's so good to see you again, Winnie, after all this time. You haven't changed a bit.' And they hugged each other for the umpteenth time and I began to wish I was with someone else.

We saw the Crown Jewels and ooohed and aaahed with the others as we filed past all too quickly. There wasn't time to stop and stare. There were always more people behind, pressing us on, and Beefeaters telling us to move along smartly. The Crown Jewels were splendid and regal enough but they looked just like the pictures I had seen of them, no better. I was impatient to get to the Bloody Tower to see where Walter Raleigh had been imprisoned, and it was already getting late. When we came out of the Crown Jewels Aunty Ellie said there'd only be time for a short visit to the Bloody Tower.

So I found myself at last inside the room where Walter Raleigh had spent thirteen years of his life. There wasn't much to see really, just a four-poster bed, a chest and a tiny window beyond.

I walked up and down Raleigh's Walk, a sort of rampart that overlooks the River Thames, and I wondered again about the old man no one else had seen at the party.

Storm clouds had gathered grey over the river and brought the evening on early. The river flowed black beyond the trees and people hurried past to be under cover before the rain came. I was alone and I was suddenly cold. Aunty Ellie and Miss Soper had gone on without me. They would wait for me outside by Tower Green, they said. They had found the Bloody Tower grim and damp, not good for her rheumatism, Aunty Ellie said. 'Don't you be too long,' she'd told me. 'We've got to get back.'

I was wondering why Walter Raleigh hadn't just made a rope out of his sheets and let himself down over the wall. It's what I would have done. I leaned over the parapet. 'Too far to jump,' said a voice from behind me. A tall figure was walking towards me, his black cloak whipping about him in the wind. He was limping, I noticed, and carried a silver-topped cane. 'So,' he said. 'So you came. Allow me to present myself.' He bowed low, sweeping his cloak across his legs. 'I am, or I was, Sir Walter Raleigh. I am your humble servant, cousin Bess.'

# CHAPTER 2

IT'S NOT BREAKING ANY SECRETS IF I TELL YOU that I am easily frightened. Moths in my hair, spiders in my bath – they make my skin crawl with fear. So you can perhaps imagine what it was like for me to see this black-wrapped spectre limping towards me. This was no dressing gown on the back of the bedroom door, no flapping curtain in the moonlight, no creaking floorboard. This was the real thing. It spoke words. It walked steps. I would have run, but I found my legs would not move. I would have screamed, but that part of me would not work either. So I fainted instead, not deliberately but willingly enough. I felt my knees buckle and my back scraping the stonework behind me as I fell. I remember the thud as my head hit the ground. There was no pain, only blackness.

Someone was calling to me from far away. 'Bess! Bess!' There was a sharp, stinging smell in my nostrils and a taste in my throat that made me cough. The stone walls of a room came out of the darkness around me and there was a beamed ceiling above me, a red-draped four-poster bed around me, and the old man's kindly face smiling down at me. I looked about me. I was in the Bloody Tower, in Sir Walter Raleigh's room. I was lying on the four-poster bed and he was sitting beside me passing a foul-smelling bottle under my nose. I pushed it away and sat up. 'Sweet cousin, believe me you have nothing to fear,' he said. 'I am, as you see, a ghost – a misfortune I have had to learn to live with. But certain it is that I mean you no harm. On the contrary, you are my dearest cousin, else I should not have appeared to you as I did.'

My voice found itself again. 'You? You are Sir Walter Raleigh?' He nodded. 'You were at the party? It was *you* at the party?' He nodded again.

'Aye,' he said. 'I am Walter Raleigh, or what is left of him.'

'But that Miss Soper, she said they cut off your head. How . . .?'

'You mean how is it that you see me now in my undamaged state?' He chuckled. 'I cannot tell you, dearest Bess, for I do not know. Faith, it is as perplexing to be a ghost as it was to be alive. But in truth, I am glad to have my head again for it was always the best part of me and, though I say it myself, many considered it a passing handsome face even in old age. What say you, cousin?' And he turned his head so that I could see his profile against the dim light of the window.

'Bess used to think my nose was quite perfect – she said as much, and often.'

'Bess?'

'Bess Throckmorton. She was my dear, dear wife,' he replied, suddenly sad. 'No man ever had such a dear sweet wife and no man ever treated a wife so cruelly. I left her behind in this world with nothing. Nothing. It hurts to say it even now, but I left my whole family with nothing.'

'But that's my name too,' I said. 'I'm Bess Throckmorton.'

He nodded.

'Indeed it is, cousin. Indeed it is, and as I told you, you are much like her, too. I miss her, I miss her to this day.' His voice hardened with anger. 'You see cousin, when they dubbed me traitor and cut off my head, they cut off my fortune too and reduced my Bess to poverty. My head they were welcome to – I had worn that long enough – but they stole my fortune and impoverished my family, and for that I shall never forgive them. One day I shall have my revenge. Mark me well, cousin. I shall be avenged.'

At that moment I heard footsteps outside the door. Walter Raleigh pulled me close to him and enveloped me in his cloak. He held me tight. 'Be still, cousin,' he whispered.

'Inside my cloak they shall not see you.'

The Beefeater was the first to come in, followed by a troop of several tourists all hung about with cameras and anoraks. 'Can't think how the door came to be shut. Always left open,' said the Beefeater. 'Anyway, here it is, the Bloody Tower, so called because it was from here in the cold light of dawn that many an unfortunate prisoner was taken down below to Tower Green for his execution. It was here in this very place that Sir Walter Raleigh spent thirteen years of his natural life.' He bent down, put his hands on his knees and spoke to the children. 'You've heard of Walter Raleigh. He was the one that laid his cloak in a puddle so Queen Elizabeth could walk across without getting her feet all muddy.'

'What did he want to do that for?' said someone, but the Beefeater ignored it and went on. 'And it was here he wrote his famous history of the world and his famous prayer the night before they cut off his head. Let me see now, how does it go? Let me see. Yes.' He cleared his throat and put his hand on his chest:

> '*Even such is time! Who takes in trust*
> *Our youth, our joys, and all we have,*
> *And pays us but with age and dust;*
> *Who, in the dark and silent grave,*
> *When we have wandered all our ways,*
> *Shuts up the story of our days!*

*But from this earth, this grave, this dust,*
*The Lord will raise me up I trust.*

'Not bad, eh, to make that up the night before you have your head cut off? Brave man he was, must have been eh? And every evening y'know he'd walk up and down the ramparts out there to stretch his legs. Raleigh's Walk we call it now.' He bent down and spoke in a hushed voice to a little boy who was sucking his finger. 'And there's some who say he still does.'

'But you haven't ever seen him, though?' said the little boy's mother quickly, more to reassure herself than her son, I thought. The little boy's eyes were wide with terror. He had his whole hand in his mouth now.

'Nope,' said the Beefeater, smiling conspiratorially and stroking his moustache, 'not myself I haven't, but I knowed someone that knowed someone else who knew a friend of his and his cousin's niece's nephew said he'd seen it.' And he boomed with laughter as they all did.

When they'd finished it was the boy's father who spoke. 'How come he was put in here anyhow?' he said. They were Americans. You could tell from their accents and their haircuts and their spongy shoes. 'After all, didn't he find America for you British? I mean, we wouldn't be speaking English if he hadn't found the good old U S of A, would we? We'd be speaking Spanish or Dutch or something. And didn't he sink lots of those Spanish galleons for you in the

Armada? And didn't he burn lots of others?'

His wife joined in. 'Yeah, and wasn't it Walter Raleigh who brought back the potatoes from Virginia and taught you British how to grow them?'

The Beefeater stroked his moustache and thought for a while. 'I believe he did, lady. I believe he did. All I know is, he was a traitor and that's why he found himself inside here. I mean he wouldn't hardly have been put in here if he was innocent, would he?' At this the Americans looked at each other and fell silent, until the little boy piped up. 'Mommy,' he said. 'It smells in here.'

'Well it *is* old, dear,' said his mother. 'Perhaps it's the damp.'

'You're right, son,' said his father, lifting his nose and sniffing the air. 'Smells just like tobacco smoke to me – cigars, perhaps.'

A tall man in spectacles at the back of the party spoke next. He was carrying a book in his hand and he spoke very deliberately and earnestly. 'In zis book it say zat Sir Valter Raleigh was ze virst man' (he wasn't an American this one, I could tell) 'who brought ze smoking of ze tobacco in England.'

'That's right, sir,' said the Beefeater. He leant down and whispered to the little boy again. 'P'raps it's old Sir Walter himself puffing away on his pipe, son. P'raps that's what you're smelling.' The boy's hand went straight back into his mouth and everyone roared with laughter, except the boy and his mother. 'Before you go, ladies and gentlemen, you'd better take the opportunity to walk up and down Raleigh's Walk a few times – it's just outside the door. It'll give you a feel of the place. Like I said, old Walter Raleigh himself used to pace up and down there every day he was here.'

But the tall bespectacled man had not yet finished. He waved his guide book in the air. 'But I do not exactly understand,' he said. 'Zey cut off his head in ze end, yes?'

'That's right sir,' said the Beefeater, trying his best to be patient.

'Zen vy did zey vait sirteen years to cut off his head? Vy did zey not cut off it at once, in ze beginning?'

'Well,' said the Beefeater. 'Well, things was different then, in them days, wasn't they? I mean if you was a king, you could change your mind when you felt like it, couldn't you? And old James the First, he just kept changing his mind. In the end he let old Sir Walter out sort of on bail. Sir Walter told the King he knew where there was this gold mine in South America, Guiana it was, and so King James sent him off to find it, but he never found it, see? And so he came back empty-handed. 'Course the King was none too pleased at that so he chopped off his head.'

'But that isn't fair,' said the little boy's father. 'Not cricket, as you British say.'

'That's true 'nough sir,' said the Beefeater. 'I suppose if you think about it, and to be honest I haven't much, but if you did think about it nothing much that happened in this place in them days was very fair. They was hard times, sir, hard times.'

'Daddy, I can still smell that smoke,' said the little boy, looking around in alarm. 'Can we go now?' And so they went, the little boy sucking his hand and looking round over his shoulder directly at me, it seemed, as he went out of the door. At last we were left alone.

Walter Raleigh left me wrapped in his black velvet cloak and limped across the room to the door. 'They've gone,' he said and he closed the door again.

'But why didn't they see us?' I asked. 'That little boy, he was looking right at me.'

'Cousin Bess, though I yearn often to be once more amongst the living, there are some advantages to be had in my present more spiritual state. Since I am but a spirit, and a spirit has no body, I may go where I will unseen. My cloak is part of me and I may hide what I will under it. I may pass through walls and doors as if they were not there, and I may eavesdrop invisibly on the living world as much as I wish – indeed there is little else to do in this wretched damp place. Oh, do not think cousin, that I do not still feel the damp in my bones. To be a ghost is to live with all the pain of the living but with little of the pleasure.'

'But I still don't understand: how can I see you and they can't?' I asked.

Sir Walter smiled. 'You can only see me because I wish you to see me. I do not wish them to see me, so they cannot. Seek to know no more, good cousin, for I know but how things are and not how they come to be so. I may tell you that I am often sorely tempted to use this ghostly talent and howl around the towers like a proper ghost, for it would certainly alarm those ignorant wretches such as the one we have just seen who have so cruelly wronged my name in history. For what is Walter Raleigh known? For laying his cloak in a puddle and for ending his days a condemned traitor. They spoke false. I was wronged, cousin; wronged, I tell you. I mind not for myself, not any more. What harm can it do me now? But I mind for my name and for my family's honour. For I never in my life betrayed my country. Indeed, I spent all my life in the loyal service of my queen and her realm. They wronged me by my death, cousin; and such a wrong should be righted – is that not so, Bess?' I nodded. 'I tell you, I cannot rest for this hurt inside me. It lingers in me like the ague that racks my bones. I would be free of it. I *will* have again what was rightly mine and what was taken so cruelly from me and my family. I will have back what is mine – mark my words, cousin.'

I shrank back from his anger and he saw that he had frightened me. He came towards me, arms outstretched to comfort me. He was dressed, I noticed, in black silk, or perhaps it was satin, I could not tell which; but it glistened even in the gloom of the room. He wore a doublet, a waistcoat and breeches, and all were black. 'I would not hurt you dear cousin, not for all the gold in the world,' he said, and he reached out his gloved hand, lifted my chin and looked into my eyes. 'I promise you, chick, Walter Raleigh is your friend and your humble servant.' And he took my hand and kissed it.

It was a little difficult to know quite what to do. I mean, no one had ever kissed my hand before. I felt suddenly like a queen or a princess and, to be honest, I liked it. He took my hand and helped me down from the bed.

'I think I'd better be going now,' I said. He looked a bit upset at this and I hated myself for my clumsiness. 'It's my Aunty Ellie,' I tried to explain. 'She'll be waiting for me down on Tower Green. She'll be wondering where I've got to and if I don't go soon she'll come looking for me. We've got to go all the way back to Devon tonight. It's a long way.'

'Devon?' said Sir Walter Raleigh, his eyes suddenly lighting up. 'Did you say Devon?'

'Yes,' I said. 'We've got a farm down in Devon, Exeter way it is, not far from Honiton. That's where I live.' He took his cloak off my shoulders and folded it over his arm. As we walked together towards the door he said nothing. He seemed deep in thought. 'I know Devon well. In truth I am, or I was, a Devon man,' he said. 'When I was a boy – and that was indeed hundreds of years ago – when I was a boy I too lived on a farm in Devon. I have dreamed of that place ever since. Perchance you know it, cousin. They call it Hayes, Hayes Barton. It lies within the parish of East Budleigh, not many miles from the sea. There never was a place more beautiful in all the world. And I should know, cousin, for I have travelled far and wide on this earth and never have I found a more pleasant place. Had I but lived out my life at Hayes, I might have kept my head on my shoulders and I might now be at peace with my soul. But what's done cannot be undone.' He stopped and put his hand on my shoulder. When I turned round and looked up, his eyes were pleading. 'Dear cousin Bess, I would I could see those green fields once again and the cows and the sheep in the meadows. I would fish once more in the silver streams and ride over the hills with the wind in my face salty from the sea. Prithee, good cousin, take me with you back to Devon. I would not trouble you for long, for a few days perhaps.' He looked around him. 'Dear God, how I tire of these grim grey walls. They were a prison for me in my life and they have been my prison ever since. There is no comfort here for my troubled spirit.'

'Bess! Bess Throckmorton!' Aunty Ellie's voice was calling from below. She was angry. She always used my surname when she was angry.

'I've really got to go,' I said and reached out to open the door. But when I turned and saw him standing alone in that cold bleak room I knew I could not leave him behind.

'Bess Throckmorton!' – Aunty Ellie again.

I opened the door. 'I'm coming!' I called out. 'All right,' I said, 'but I don't think anyone at home would like the idea of a ghost in the house. They wouldn't understand, and my Gran's got a bad heart. If she gets upset she has one of her turns, so you've got to promise you won't ever show yourself. It'll be a secret, just you and me, no one else.'

'I would not have it any other way, dear cousin,' said Walter Raleigh, his face beaming with joy. 'We shall bind ourselves now in a solemn promise. I shall not reveal myself to anyone except to you and in return you shall tell no one of this meeting or of your cousin Walter. They would only think you mad – and I would not have anyone believe that of you. I will be your true and secret friend, dear Bess, for as long as you have need of me. You have my word on it.'

'Bess Throckmorton!'

'I shall follow you, cousin. You will not always see me, for I find it tires me to show myself for too long, but rest assured that I shall be at your side.'

As I came down the steps I noticed that Aunty Ellie and Miss Soper were talking to the same Beefeater I had seen showing the tourists round the Bloody Tower. I called out to Aunty Ellie because I had a sudden terrible sinking feeling that she might not be able to see me, that no one would ever see me again. I was quite relieved when she looked up and saw me. 'Bess!' she cried, rushing towards me. 'Bess Throckmorton! Whatever have you been up to? Where have you been?'

'Nothing,' I said, shrugging my shoulders. 'Nowhere.'

'I was just telling this gentleman here how I left you up there and he swore blue murder there was no one else up there.' The Beefeater she was talking about came over to join us. 'You see,' Aunty Ellie said to him pointedly. 'She *was* up there, just like I said. I told you, didn't I?'

The Beefeater looked at me and frowned. He was more than a little puzzled. 'Well, I just don't understand it, lady,' he protested. 'I don't understand it at all. I was up there not five minutes ago and I'm telling you there was no one up there. Hiding under the bed were you? You're not s'posed to go near that bed. They do that, these kids, sometimes. Got no discipline these days.'

'I was out on Raleigh's Walk,' I said. 'Down the end.'

'I never seen you,' said the Beefeater.

'Well wherever you were you took a mighty long time about it,' said Aunty Ellie. 'Worried me sick, you did. And Winnie has very likely caught a cold waiting out here for you. Most inconsiderate, Bess Throckmorton. I'm surprised at you. Now come along. We've to drop Winnie off at her hotel and then we must get back to Devon. I promised your mother I'd have you back home by midnight.'

And so we were. I sat in the front all the way but I could not resist looking over my shoulder into the back seat. Sir

Walter Raleigh was there. I could not see him but I knew he was there. Somehow I could feel him, and more than once Aunty Ellie had to open a window. 'I smell cigarette smoke,' she said, tutting and shaking her head. 'Must've been Winnie. I never knew she smoked. It clings to the clothes, you know. Filthy habit. Never smoke, Bessy dear, you hear me, never. Can't think why anyone ever invented the filthy habit.'

Mother noticed it too, as I climbed into bed that night. 'Better wash your hair tomorrow,' she said as she kissed me goodnight. 'It smells of cigarette smoke. 'Spect there were lots of people smoking at the party, were there?' I nodded. 'Did you meet anyone interesting?' Mindful of who was probably listening, I replied: 'Just one.'

'Who was he?'

'He's called Walter,' I said. And Mother went out. I heard her talking to Father in the passage outside the bathroom later. 'She met a friend called Walter,' she said.

'Boyfriends already,' said Father. 'Funny name, Walter,' and their bedroom door closed.

'Are you there, Sir Walter?' I whispered.

'I'm here.' The voice came first, then the cloaked figure appeared sitting in the chair under the mantelpiece where I kept my collection of china owls.

'Where you going to sleep?' I asked.

'Like your owls, ghosts don't sleep much,' he said. He leaned heavily on his cane and stood up. 'Good night, dear cousin, and may God bless you always for your kindness to me. I shall not forget it.' And he came over to my bed, took my hand and kissed it gently.

'Goodnight, Sir Walter,' I said.

'I am called Walter to my friends and family. You are indeed my family and I trust you will always be my friend.'

'Yes,' I said. And my friend Walter walked out through the door and was gone as suddenly as he had come. Downstairs Humph began to bark furiously and to scratch at the back door, and only I knew it wasn't the fox he was after.

# CHAPTER 3

LIVING WITH A GHOST HAS ITS DIFFICULTIES, I discovered, even if he is your friend. Of course I knew he would be as good as his word and not appear suddenly out of nowhere and frighten Gran half to death; but it was disconcerting, to say the least, not to know if he was in the room with you or whether he was listening in. It would be, he said, far too tiring for him to show himself to me all the time, and it was true that if he appeared too often and for too long he would become hazy at the edges. It seems ghosts need time to recharge themselves, so to speak.

So between us we had to devise a code, an exchange of signals. I would cough twice – that was to ask if he was there – and if he was he would open a door, or drop something on the floor. Much to my disappointment he never seemed to use china or glass for this. More often it was a pencil or a newspaper that fell casually off a table, to Humph's great delight. He would pounce at once and carry it off in triumph either to bury it somewhere or to chew it to pieces in his basket. But if I wanted Walter actually to appear, we agreed I would cough four times. It would work out well enough, we thought – just so long as I didn't develop a real cough. Of course all this secrecy, all these signals, were really more for Gran's benefit than anyone else's. I didn't dare think what might happen if she ever found out about Walter.

But find out she very nearly did. She couldn't walk very easily because of her 'creaky knees' as she called them; and she couldn't see very well, on account of her reading too much in the dark when she was little, she said; but her ears worked perfectly, too perfectly at times, for it was Gran who said she'd overheard me talking in my room one evening. I said I must have been talking to myself.

'She's always talked to herself, Gran,' said Mother, 'ever since she was little. Bess has been telling herself stories ever since she could talk, you know that.'

'Yes, but then I heard a man's voice,' Gran went on. 'Clear as daylight, it was.'

'I probably had my radio on,' I said. I'm quite good at thinking quickly when I have to.

'Well, it didn't sound like a wireless to me,' Gran said. And luckily an argument developed as to whether a wireless should be called a wireless any more, or whether it should be a radio or a transistor; and the question of a man's voice in my room was forgotten. It was too close for comfort though, so my friend Walter and I decided that in future we should talk in the house only in an emergency, and then always in a whisper.

As it turned out, though, it was Humph not Gran who proved to be the greatest danger. Humph seemed to be able to sense Walter's presence whenever he was in the room, and he would stiffen, hackles raised, and set up a furious barking with intermittent thunderous growling. Once or twice he even bared his teeth – something he had never been known to do before. No one could understand it. At first they put it down to the fact that Will was still away at camp, and that perhaps Humph was missing him. Mother became so worried she called in the vet who examined Humph carefully and pronounced that he might have a middle ear infection, causing him to lose his balance and hear things that weren't there. So poor old Humph had to have drops poured down his ear three times a day.

In the end though I managed to find a way around even this problem. I 'borrowed' some scraps of meat from the larder and I told Walter that the only way to Humph's heart was through his stomach, which was quite true. So now Walter would appear from time to time and offer him some meat scraps, and of course he soon had him eating out of his hand. But I'm afraid this didn't work out exactly as I had intended. Now, whenever Humph smelt or perhaps sensed my friend Walter was anywhere near, he would wag his tail enthusiastically. Of course that caused a draught which would make Gran's ankles cold and so he would often find himself inexplicably put out of the door. Poor Humph. It wasn't fair.

Mother was delighted, though, with Humph's apparent recovery, and full of praise for the young vet. She went on and on about how clever he had been in his diagnosis. 'Wait for the bill,' was all Father said.

Father seemed somehow preoccupied and sombre all this time, quite unlike himself. I thought it was because Will was away at first – they got on like a house on fire, those two. They laughed at the same jokes, and were always off rabbiting and fishing together. He liked me, too, of course, but not quite in the same easy way; and I always wished he would. I didn't mind quite so much now because I had a friend of my own – and what a time we had the two of us.

It was like letting a bird out of a cage. Walter wanted to see everything, go everywhere and do everything. First he wanted to go fishing. So I lent him Will's fishing rod and we spent long hours together down by the river that runs through the marsh field at the bottom of the farm. We'd be alone there. Just so long as I kept an eye out for the 'horrible Barrowbills', we could talk freely. (The Barrowbill brothers – identical twins – farmed on the other side of the river. 'The

Horrible Barrowbills', we always called them – horrible because they were always shouting at us if they found us on their side of the river. They even fired a shot at Humph once to frighten him away.) But horrible or not, they never came near Walter and me.

Once Walter had mastered the complexities of Will's reel he fished like an expert, delighting in every catch and cursing his 'devilish luck' if he ever let one off the hook, and that wasn't often. He built a small fire and cooked two of the fish in the hot ashes for me. I tell you, nothing had ever tasted that good to me before. But our fishing expedition got me into dangerous difficulties at home.

It came as a bit of a surprise to Father when I brought back a bag full of sea trout. 'What's come over you, Bess?' he said. 'You've never shown any interest in fishing before.' I could tell he was quite impressed and it seemed for a moment to lift him out of his gloom. 'I'll come down with you one night,' he said. 'River's just right for sea trout. Shy fish, your sea trout. Best to go after him in the dark, but I'm a bit tied up just at the moment.' And I saw glances exchanged between him and Mother. Something was wrong, I knew it was; but I had neither the time nor the inclination to worry about it. I was far too busy looking after my friend Walter.

Next he wanted to go riding – he insisted on it. I did my best to discourage him because Sally hadn't been ridden for a while and she could play up a bit with an inexperienced rider.

'She can be awful wicked,' I said. 'She'll run away with you if you're not careful. She's done it before. And what if the horrible Barrowbills see you, anyway?'

'You forget that we spirits have our ways,' he said. 'All they'll see is a galloping horse. They'll not see me, not unless I want them to. And I'll not show myself to anyone except you, remember?' Walter showed himself more often these days. He said he found the country air invigorating, that it didn't tire him so much to show himself now as it had done back in the Tower.

So no one saw Walter riding out on Sally except me, and I saw them both as they thundered past through the high thistles, with Walter bent low over Sally's neck, his cloak whipping about behind him. Herons and ducks lifted off in alarm as they galloped towards the river, and I could see from the way Sally moved that she was enjoying being ridden. She was collected and controlled. She was being ridden by a real horseman and she knew it.

Afterwards we swam in the river together and lay on the bank in the sun. Walter smoked his pipe and he talked and talked, as if he'd had no one to talk to for hundreds of years.

'I have had an eternity, cousin, an eternity now to think on the errors of my ways, and they were many and unforgivable. I see now, dear cousin, and for the first time too, that my gravest error was ever to leave the farm and the countryside.'

'Why did you leave, then?' I asked.

'I did not wish it,' he sighed. 'I was sent away from home as were all young men of rank in those days. I went to Oxford first, but I cared neither for books nor the grey men of the cloisters who were my tutors, and I left for the wars. That's what a young man did if he wanted to make his mark in this world. And I wanted to make my mark, cousin.'

'What do you mean?' I asked.

Walter wasn't always easy to understand and he seemed to know it. 'I speak of ambition, cousin. Walter Raleigh had to be great in the land, he had to be powerful, and rich and admired. And to be that he had to go to Court. And so I went to Court and was noticed at last by good Queen Bess, Queen Elizabeth; and she favoured me with her love and her attention.'

'Was that when you spread your cloak in the puddle for her?' I asked. He nodded and smiled.

'That was the start of it, I grant you. I was always one for the grand gesture. So I became Captain of her guard and was soon rich beyond dreams, as powerful almost as the queen herself. Truly, cousin, the world was at my feet. Then I met and married Bess Throckmorton, your ancestor and my dear wife, and she won my heart. She was suddenly more important to me than all the world, all the gold and all the glory. But the queen would not have it.'

'Couldn't you marry who you wanted to?' I asked.

'Aye, so long as the queen wanted it too, and she did not want it. I think she would not have minded if I had not loved Bess so well. But she knew I did and that made her mad with me. She sent me to the Tower.'

'Is that why they cut off your head, because you married someone she didn't like?'

Walter laughed. 'No sweet cousin, no; but I was never again to be so high in the esteem of my queen, nor never again so high in the land.'

'So why did she cut off your head?'

' 'Twas not the Queen that destroyed me.' His brow lowered as he went on. ' 'Twas the monstrous king that followed her – King James. He it was that had me tried for high treason and condemned as a traitor – Walter Raleigh a traitor!' His eyes blazed. 'And 'twas this same villainous king who robbed my family of all we had. He it was that took away my lands, and my farms and estates – even the jewels from my fingers. Yet I blame myself as much as the King, for there was more pride in my head than wisdom; and right it was it should be struck off, for I had grievously mismanaged my affairs through a mistaken belief in my own invincibility, a belief that led not to riches but to the death of my son, my dear Wat. He was a rebellious boy and argued much, but I loved him nonetheless. And 'twas I who caused his death.' And he turned his head away from me to wipe his eyes.

'What d'you mean?' I asked.

'They let me out of the Tower only because I said I knew of a gold mine in Guiana that would fill the King's coffers.'

'That's what the Beefeater said in the Tower,' I said, but he did not seem to hear me.

'I knew where the gold mine was, but by the time we reached Guiana I was too ill to lead the expedition. So I sent Wat in my place, and the Spaniards were waiting for him in the forests. They were informed, I tell you, cousin, and by no less a person than the king himself. I know it to be so. They ambushed my men and so came my son to his death, our expedition to its failure and my life to its miserable end on the scaffold.' He shook his head and sighed deeply. 'Dear God, I can scarcely bear to think on it even now. So you see, cousin, where vain ambition leads. I should have stayed on the farm where I belonged. But look!'

He put his hand on my arm. A heron circled above us and came in to land at the water's edge not a stone's throw away. As he watched him stalking stiffly through the shallows, a kingfisher flashed past us and was gone again upstream. 'Such wonders as these I had almost forgotten,' he whispered, and the heron lifted off and lumbered into the air.

And it was not only in the wild creatures of the farm that he found such joy. He made a collection of many of the plants and herbs and flowers he found about the farm, though at the time I did not know why. In the warm summer evenings he would walk with me through the fields of humming clover amongst the sheep and the cattle and recall his own days as a boy on the farm. The fields were bigger now, he said, and there were fewer trees, and he could wish the river was clearer again and the meadows full with wild flowers as they had been once. But that apart, it was much as he remembered it. I showed him how I liked to follow butterflies and he loved it as much as I did. We followed one Red Admiral for a whole afternoon once before it joined up with a dozen others on a bank of nettles. After that we couldn't be sure which was ours and we lost it.

He was fascinated too by the farm machinery, the mower, the four-furrow plough, the baler, the hay-elevator and the corn-drill. He wanted me to explain the working of each one, and I found that difficult, for although I loved driving the tractor I had never much interested myself in how the farm machines actually worked.

It was the tractor in particular that took his fancy. If I do nothing else remarkable in my life it will be enough to claim that I, Bess Throckmorton, taught Sir Walter Raleigh to drive a tractor. Cars he said were 'but insects compared with the majesty of a tractor'.

One misty morning I drove the little Massey Ferguson 125 (the only one Father would let me drive) to the little meadow below the wood where no one could see us, and Walter climbed up into the seat. I showed him what was what and off he went, his laughter ringing above the chugging and spluttering of the engine. He made figures of eight through the long grass and then rumbled away down towards the gate to the marsh field and the river beyond. I called for him to come back, for the 'horrible Barrowbills' might well have been fishing on the far bank, and to them or to anyone else the sight of a tractor driving itself along might be a little upsetting (not that I minded upsetting the Barrowbills, but there would be bound to be telephone calls and questions and difficult explanations). Anyway, Walter obediently turned and at full throttle bore down on me, his black cloak flying out behind him. It occurred to me for a moment he might forget what he was riding and where the brake was, that he might be expecting the 125 to rear up on its hind legs and paw the air and whinny. He was riding it just like a horse. But he stopped it in time and patted it on the chimney. It took all my persuasive powers to get him off so that I could drive it back to the sheds, but in the end he rode up beside me on the step and laughed like a boy all the way home.

We made hay until dark that evening – all of us there. Mother turning and Father baling, and Walter and me standing them up in castles of four in case of rain. Gran kept bringing out the orange juice and the tea and the buns and grumbled about her creaky knees (she could be an old misery sometimes) and Mother kept telling me not to lift the heavy ones. 'Bad for your back,' she said. 'They're lighter in the middle of the field. I'll manage the wet ones along the hedges.' But of course she need not have worried, for I had all the help I needed that evening. Hay bales had never felt so light to me.

'You're working well Bess,' Father called out. 'We'll make a farmer of you yet!' And I glowed inside. I had a sudden longing to introduce him to my friend Walter. I wanted very much for them to like each other, but a secret is a secret and I kept it. I was hot and I was dusty and I was tired, but at that moment I was as happy as any lark. Why is it, though, that the good times never seem to last for long?

Will returned home later that night, and came and sat on my bed and talked about the miles they had tramped, the mountains they had climbed, the secret cigarettes he had smoked, and all about Peter Munns from school who had fallen out of a tree and broken his leg, and how it served him right anyway. But, to be fair to Will, it wasn't his coming home that spoiled everything. To be honest, I was quite pleased to have him home again. He kept everyone happy and he made everyone laugh. Even Father cheered up a bit. I don't like to admit it but if truth be told we need Will in our house. He's the glue that sticks us all together, if you know what I mean.

'Did you go to that party with Aunt Ellie?' he asked after he'd finished telling me all about his camp.

'Went to the Tower of London,' I said.

'See the Crown Jewels? Wicked, aren't they?'

'I saw the Bloody Tower,' I said, 'where Sir Walter Raleigh lived. He's a distant relation of ours, you know.'

'Relation?'

'Ancestor then.'

'How d'you know?'

'Aunty Ellie said, so did Miss Soper.'

'Who's she?'

'Cousin of Aunty Ellie's.'

'I done him in history.'

'Who?'

'Walter Raleigh. When we did the Armada at school. Had his head cut off, didn't he? Traitor, wasn't he?'

'No he wasn't!'

'Well they cut off his head, didn't they? Must've done something wrong.'

'They shouldn't have done. He didn't do anything wrong.'

I might have said more than I meant to if the argument had had a chance to get going. But it didn't. There were sudden loud voices downstairs in the kitchen. We looked at each other, Will and I. We could hear Father banging the table and shouting.

'What's up with them?' Will asked. 'Arguing about Gran are they?'

It's true that Gran was the only thing they ever argued about, and that was rare enough. 'Don't think so,' I said. 'Father's not been like himself. Something's wrong, I think, but I don't know what.' I had a sudden tickle in my throat, it must have been from the hay dust. I coughed twice. My blue elephant fell off the chest of drawers and landed at Will's feet. I spoke without thinking. 'I didn't mean it like that,' I said, and then I clapped my hand to my mouth.

'Didn't mean what like what?' Will asked as he picked up Elephant. 'What are you on about?' And he pulled Elephant's trunk and tied it into a knot like he always did.

'Nothing,' I said, bouncing out of bed and snatching it out of his hand. 'Didn't mean nothing.' But Will was canny and he knew when I was lying. He always did.

'You're up to something, Bessy,' he said, looking around him. 'What little mystery have you been hatching up in here while I've been away?'

'Nothing. Don't know what you mean.'

'We'll see,' he said and went towards the door. He stopped and sniffed the air. 'Smells of tobacco in here. You been smoking, have you?' I shook my head vigorously. He sniffed again. 'Funny,' he said. 'And there's another thing, you've been down in my chemistry lab, haven't you?'

'No.'

'You sure?'

'Course I haven't. I hate your smelly chemistry lab. Anyway I never go down the cellar. I'm frightened silly of the spiders. You know I am.'

He seemed to accept that. 'Well, someone's been down

there, that's all I know,' he said. 'Someone's been down there messing about. I know they have.'

'Well, it wasn't me,' I said, knowing quite well who it was. Who else could it have been? Will seemed satisfied with that and he went out leaving the door open. He always left my door open. I shut it and listened to be sure that he was gone. I coughed four times and nothing happened, not at first.

'You there, Walter?' I whispered. And he appeared just where I thought he was, sitting in my chair. He seemed to like my chair. 'It was you wasn't it? You've been down in his chemistry lab, haven't you? Why? What for?'

He held up his hands and chuckled. 'I confess it freely, chick,' he said. I liked it when he called me 'chick'. 'You must excuse me but I have a passion for a knowledge of science, and for chemistry in particular. I was a man of science in my lifetime and did many experiments with plants and herbs and, though I say it myself, I was not entirely unsuccessful. Science to me is like the world – there is much to explore, much to discover. One gains such a paltry slice of knowledge in just one lifetime.' He bowed his head. 'Your pardon cousin. Henceforth I shall not indulge myself without greater caution. That much I promise.'

'It's not going to be so easy now that Will's back,' I said. 'And you'd better stop smoking in the house. He's suspicious already. I know he is.'

'If you say I must not, then I will not.'

'He's cunning as a weasel, eyes in the back of his head,' I said.

'What a weasel cannot see a weasel cannot catch,' said Walter. 'Do not trouble yourself, sweet Bess. All will be well.'

But I knew my big brother Will a lot better than he did, and I wasn't quite so sure.

# CHAPTER 4

NOW THAT WILL WAS BACK HOME I SEEMED TO see less and less of my friend Walter. That's not to say that he wasn't there. He was, but not so often. Before he had stayed by me almost all day and every day. I only had to cough to be sure he was there. But more and more now my coughing signals brought no response and I began to wonder where he was and what he was doing on his own.

It didn't help that when he was with me we could no longer be sure of being alone anywhere. However hard we tried, Walter and I could not lose ourselves for very long. Somehow, wherever we went Will would appear sooner or later, and all too often he had caught me talking to myself, or so he thought. This everlasting game of hide-and-seek upset both Walter and me. Perhaps that was why he stayed away. I made every effort to winkle out of Walter what he did when he was alone – I was curious, that's all – but the most he ever revealed was in these few cryptic words: 'A ghost knows well enough how to pass the time,' he said. 'He's had time enough to learn.' And he said no more. However, I was to find out soon enough how my friend Walter was passing his time.

One morning just before breakfast Will came storming into the kitchen waving his fishing rod like a weapon. He was crying with rage. 'Who said you could borrow my rod?' I gaped at him. He appealed to Mother. 'Look what she's gone and done. The line's all caught up and the reel's jammed.'

'I never touched it,' I protested. Right away I knew who the culprit was. 'Honest I never. I haven't been fishing since you came back.'

'P 'raps your father took it,' said Mother, trying to calm the storm. 'You'd better ask him before you go accusing your sister like that.'

'I *have* asked him,' Will shouted. 'And he told me he's been too busy to go anywhere near the river for weeks. It was you. Couldn't be anyone else, could it?' And he waved the rod in my face.

'I never touched your silly rod,' I screamed, knocking it aside. 'Only that once while you were away. I didn't think you'd mind, just once.'

'I'm not talking about then, am I?' Will said. 'You messed

up my rod, and you're going to pay for it. The whole thing's jammed solid.'

At that very moment Gran came in from the pantry carrying a plate and on the plate were four gleaming silver trout. 'Well someone's been fishing,' she said. 'And I can tell you it's not me. Fresh as daisies, these are. Found them on the kitchen table when I came down this morning. Straight out of the river, I'd say.' She put the plate down on the table and wagged her finger at me. 'I've told you before, Bess. Neither a borrower nor a lender be.' And she had told me – often. It was one of her little sayings – Gran had hundreds of them and she trotted them out whenever she could.

Father came in from milking and kicked off his boots by the door. 'What's all the fuss about?' he said. 'You two been at each other's throats again?' And Will told him the whole story and pointed in triumph to the plate of fish on the table. He picked it up and carried it across the kitchen and presented it to Father as evidence. 'Sea trout again – couple of pounds each. Nice fish. Well?' Father said, looking down at me. 'What have you got to say to this, my girl? Could hardly catch 'em without a rod, could you?' There was nothing for it but to confess. I made the best of it I could.

'I thought you'd like the fish, that's all,' I cried. 'You're always saying money's short and we've got to go careful, and so I thought I'd try and catch a few fish.' And the tears flowed as freely as I could manage.

'She didn't mean any harm, Will,' said Mother, putting her arm around me and drying my eyes with the dishcloth.

'All right,' said Will. 'But she's got to ask, that's all, or get her own. What am I going to do about this line? I'll never get it undone.'

'I'll give you a hand with it later, Will,' said Father, and he ruffled my hair. 'You went out and caught these?' he asked. 'Last night?' I nodded. 'Should've been in bed, shouldn't you?' There was some consolation at least in the admiring look he gave me, but things were getting out of hand and I knew I'd have to speak to my friend Walter, and soon.

I found him that evening out in Sally's field. I'd been coughing for him everywhere, increasingly angry at the predicament he had landed me in. When I told him he just roared with laughter. 'I commend you, Bess, for your quick wit,' he said. And then he went on. 'Did you see the moon last night, chick?'

'I was asleep last night,' I said, wondering what that had to do with anything.

'Had you seen the moon, and the mist rising from the valley floor, you could not have stayed abed.' Walter went on. 'Fish rise on such a night, dearest cousin. I could not but go. And what a night it was, filled with the cries of owls and foxes, and the piping and splashing of otters. On such a night a soul can be at peace – even one such as mine.'

'How did you mess up his reel?' I asked.

'Alas, I became entwined with an unfortunate overhanging branch,' he said. 'One of the perils of fishing at night. I did all I could, cousin. I climbed the tree to retrieve it, and that was no easy task for a ghost of my years. Despite my best endeavours however I ended up with a bird's nest for a reel and had to come home. I ask you, what was I to do? Was I to leave the fish I had caught for the otters and the herons? I wanted to keep them for you, so that we might cook them again by the river as we did once before, remember? Would you scold me for that, dear cousin? I brought them back for you. I was in the kitchen with the fish laid out on the table and trying to unravel the infernal line, when the door opened.'

'Gran?'

He nodded. 'She made at once for the stove to put on the kettle for her morning tea. She always rises with the birds for her cup of tea, and I had forgotten it. She took one look at the fish and straightway scooped them up and set about washing them and gutting them. I thought it best not to steal them away from under her nose. The shock of such a thing I thought might indeed have grave consequences. So there you have it all, cousin. I own the fault was mine, and if I have harmed you, dear Bess, then I beg you humbly to forgive your wretched cousin, who loves you tenderly and would have you love him as well.' How could I be angry with him for long? 'Am I forgiven, cousin?'

'I suppose so, but we'd better not pinch his rod again, that's all,' I said. 'I'll see if I can borrow Father's for you from time to time if you want. He likes me to go fishing – he won't mind.'

Walter became suddenly thoughtful. He looked out across the fields to the hills beyond and patted Sally's neck. 'I think I shall not be fishing for some time, cousin,' he said. 'There is somewhere I have to go. There is something that must be done.'

'What do you mean? Where are you going?' I asked, but he never replied. I thought he had not heard me. 'Will you be gone for long?' I asked.

'Fear not, dear Bess,' he said, putting his arm around me. 'I shall be back and soon. You can count on it.'

Looking back now I should have foreseen what would happen. The very next day Sally went missing. Gran was the last to see her. She had seen her first thing in the morning when she went to fill up her water bucket as usual. (Gran loved Sally, and in spite of her creaky knees always took it upon herself to look after Sally in the summer time. She said the regular exercise would do her good). I did not know anything about it until the afternoon when I came back from the dentist with Mother. There was a police car in the yard. Father broke the news. 'Sally's disappeared,' he said. 'She's worth over a thousand pounds to me, that mare. It's a sound fence, I tell you. She couldn't have got out, not on her own. She's been taken, I know she has.'

'What, in broad daylight?' said the policeman, who looked hot in his uniform and kept wiping his neck with his handkerchief. 'Hardly likely, sir.'

'There's been no one here most of the day. Would've been easy,' Father went on.

'Well of course we'll keep an eye out for her, sir,' said the policeman, 'but I think you'll find she'll come trotting up the road before the evening's out. P'raps someone left the gate open.' And everyone looked at Gran who was almost in tears.

But Sally never did come home that evening, nor the next, nor the next. Of course I knew who'd taken her. I went out around the farm coughing for Walter. I even risked shouting for him. But I knew it was no good even as I was doing it. I went everywhere we'd been together, into the tractor sheds, down to the river, along the marsh field, into the meadow; but he'd gone and I knew well enough who he'd taken with him on his travels.

No one actually blamed Gran, not in so many words, but the trouble was no one had seen a van or a horsebox coming up the farm lane that day and the field did not open out on to the road. It was difficult to see how Sally could have been stolen without someone seeing something, and if Sally had not been stolen, there could only be one other explanation. Somehow the gate must have been left open. But then, as Father said, someone must have shut it because he'd found the gate closed. Horses don't shut gates after themselves, he said. He was still sure she'd been taken.

But Gran blamed herself anyway, whatever anyone said. As the days passed and Sally didn't come back she became more and more upset. Everyone tried to console her, even Father, and he wasn't always that kind to Gran. 'It wasn't your fault, Gran, I know it wasn't,' I heard him tell her. 'She's been stolen, must've been: but you never know, they may still find her, she's got a brand on her after all. Don't you worry, Gran.' But Gran shook her head and plunged deeper and deeper into silent misery. Aunty Ellie came in every day and sat by her to cheer her up, but that didn't seem to help much. She wouldn't even eat Aunty Ellie's walnut cake – usually her favourite. She just didn't seem interested in going on living.

It was a fortnight later – the first day of the new school year, I remember – that Gran had one of her turns and the doctor was called out. He said that if she wasn't any better by the next day then she'd have to go into hospital. That same evening after I'd had my tea I was out picking blackberries in Front Meadow and I heard a horse snorting. I turned around. Sally was standing under the shade of the chestnut tree at the bottom of her field. She was grazing peacefully and hardly bothered to look up as I approached. She had sweated up I noticed, but she was groomed nicely, and when I lifted her feet up I could see that they were picked clean. 'Where have you been, Sally?' I said.

'With me,' said a voice from behind. Walter was standing there leaning on his cane, a wicked half-smile on his face. 'Well, dear cousin, are you not pleased to see me? Have you not missed me sorely?'

My anger boiled instantly and explosively. 'You steal my father's horse. You go away for days and days without saying a word. Do you know what you've gone and done? You've nearly killed my Gran, that's what you've done. She thought she'd left the gate open by mistake and let Sally out, and now she's had one of her turns worrying about it. You don't *think*! You don't care about other people. It may just be a ghostly game to you and we may be just puppets you play with, but I'll never speak to you again, never.' I was steamed up and would not stop now. 'They were right to cut off your head. They were. You can go back to your Bloody Tower and rot there for all I care.' And I ran off.

They thought I was crying with relief when I burst into the house and told them about Sally. They came running out to see for themselves. Walter was nowhere to be seen as Sally came trotting over towards the house to greet us.

But the glad news did not seem to help Gran. That evening she refused her supper again and turned her face to the wall. In the kitchen the five of us sat around the table – even Little Jim seemed quiet and dejected.

'Can't understand it,' said Father, shaking his head. 'A horse can't just go off and come back like as if it's been on holiday or something. Can't understand it at all.'

'You should shoot her,' said Will vehemently.

'Will!' said Mother.

'Well, if Gran dies it'll be Sally that killed her,' said Will, wiping away his tears with his grubby hands.

'Wasn't Sally's fault,' I said, before I could stop myself; and they all looked at me at once. I thought then of blurting the whole thing out, but they'd never have believed it anyway. Will would have scoffed at me and my Mother and Father would think it was just one of my stories; and it was true, I *was* always telling them stories. They never really believed them and I knew they didn't, but I went on telling them just the same. I wasn't a liar, exactly. I just liked making up stories, and this one they would certainly never believe, not in a million years. Well, who would?

'If it wasn't Sally that brought on her turn it would've been something else,' said Mother. 'The doctor says we had to expect this sometime. There's no sense in getting all het up. She won't die, Will. She'll come through it, I know she will.' She gripped Father's hand on the table. 'She will, won't she?' she said to him, and she buried her head in his shoulder. Father waved us out of the room and we went outside, Will still wiping his eyes. He put his arm around my shoulder. 'She'll be all right,' he said. 'She's got to be.' I decided I quite liked my brother after all.

I was lying on my bed before I noticed the note on my

bedside table, and on top of it was a small bottle. The writing was difficult to read, the letters tall and regular but strangely formed. I could read it only slowly.

*Dearest Cousin,*

*I have wronged you and your family most dreadfully, and your anger towards me was deserved and your hatred justifiably fierce. I do deserve no better. I ask no pardon, but to say that all I did I did for you as I trust you will one day discover. I pray you make haste to administer the elixir in the bottle to your grandmother. Delay not for I fear she has dire need of it. A few drops in her tea will suffice for a full recovery. Do it now and you will see my time spent collecting plants and herbs and all the hours in your brother's laboratory were not entirely wasted.*

*Your humble and most affectionate cousin,*

*W.R.*

The liquid in the bottle was of a dark, mushy green colour, as much like pond water as anything else. I did not think twice about it. I put it at once into my skirt pocket and made my way along the corridor to Gran's room. I went on tip-toe as the kitchen was right below, and I could hear Mother still sobbing quietly and Father trying to comfort her.

Gran lay propped up on a bank of pillows, her face as white as her hair. Her eyes were closed. The tea was still warm in the cup by her bed. She had not drunk any. As I tried to release a few drops the bottle trembled in my hand and too much came out all at once.

'Come on, Gran,' I whispered, shaking her shoulder gently. Her eyes opened. 'You've got to have a cup of tea. You know you like a nice cup of tea.' She shook her head. 'It'll do you good. I made it specially for you. "Waste not, want not". That's what you always tell me, remember.' A suggestion of a smile moved her lips and that was enough to encourage me. I put my arm around her neck and helped her to drink it down. She spilt some down her nightie, but she took almost half a cup before she fell back against the pillows. 'That was nice, dear,' she said. And she closed her eyes again. I left her and went back to my bedroom. I opened the bottle and smelt it. It smelt like minty cough mixture. I pondered again and again over the note. I do not know why, but I had absolute and complete faith in my friend Walter. I never doubted, not for one minute, that his medicine, his 'elixir', would work.

It couldn't have been more than an hour later when I heard Gran calling from her room. Will raced along the passage outside my door. Mother and Father were taking the stairs in twos with Humph close on their heels. By the time I reached Gran's room they were all there. I was not at all surprised at what I saw. Gran was sitting up in her bed, her face still pale but her eyes bright and alert.

'I had the strangest dream,' she said looking somewhat

bemused. 'There was this old man bending over me. Dressed all in black he was, and with a handsome beard on him. He had earrings just like a pirate. I don't usually like men with earrings. It's not proper. Anyway, he told me I'd be quite all right just so long as I drank a cup of tea; and then he disappeared, vanished into thin air. Then soon after in comes Bess – it was you, dear, wasn't it?'

'Yes, Gran,' I said.

'I thought so. And she told me to drink a cup of tea and so I did, and I'm right as rain now.' Mother and Father and Will looked at each other in utter amazement. 'I could eat a horse,' Gran said, smiling, 'honest I could.'

'Sally perhaps?' said Will, and we all laughed or cried – it was difficult to tell which.

Again and again that night I coughed for my friend Walter, so much so that Mother came in to give me some cough medicine in the early hours. 'You've been coughing a lot lately,' she said. The cough linctus made me feel very sleepy, but I forced myself to stay awake. I tried calling him softly by name. 'Walter! Sir Walter!' But he never came. 'I didn't mean it, Walter,' I said as sleep overcame me. 'Honest I didn't. Come back, please come back.'

But he never came. I had banished my best friend, my only friend, and I had only myself to blame.

# CHAPTER 5

DOCTOR RODERICK CAME FIRST THING THE NEXT morning, an old man with more hair growing out of his ears than on his head.

'Remarkable,' he said shaking his head as he came downstairs into the kitchen. 'She's as bright as a button. Quite remarkable.' And he patted me on the head as he passed by. 'You got her to take a cup of tea, your Mother tells me, Bess.' I nodded. 'Must've been something you put in it,' he said, and everyone laughed except me. Little Jim squawked in his chair and bit harder on the edge of his bowl. 'Still teething is he, Mrs Throckmorton?' the doctor asked.

'He's got six now,' said Mother proudly.

'Six of his very own,' said the doctor. 'Well, that's

splendid. Splendid. That's more than I have now, you know. A fine-looking boy you've got there Mr Throckmorton. Make a good farmer by the look of him.'

Father nodded. 'That's if there's anything left to farm, doctor,' he said.

'Hard times, eh?' said the doctor.

'Could be better,' said Father.

'Still, you've got your health,' the doctor said. 'And that's the main thing. Without your health you can't do anything.'

'I suppose so, Doctor,' said Father, but he did not sound convinced. The doctor sat down at the table beside me and wrote out a prescription. 'She's to take this four times a day, and she's to stay in bed,' he said. 'And lots more of your tea, Bess. She needs lots of liquids.' I smiled weakly.

'Bess has got a bit of a cough, Doctor,' said Mother. 'Been coming on for some time. She was coughing all night last night, weren't you dear?'

'Better have a look at it then, whilst I'm here,' said the doctor. And he got me to say 'aaah', and put a lolly stick on my tongue and peered deep into my mouth. He had lots of little purple veins all over his nose. 'Looks healthy enough to me,' he said after a moment or two. 'Need some of your own medicine perhaps, Bess. The dust from the hay I shouldn't wonder. A good cup of tea will help.' He smiled at me. And sure enough his teeth were far too white and too even to be real. I'd never noticed before. Still, I thought, there's not many people who admit to having false teeth. Gran would die if you even mentioned hers.

Father accompanied the doctor to the door. 'I've got to go to the bank this afternoon,' he said, 'so I'll pick up the prescription when I'm in town.'

'Soon as you can,' said the doctor, and he was gone. Mother sent me upstairs a few minutes later with Gran's breakfast tray. As I went past my room I noticed the door was open. I always shut it to keep Humph off my bed. Someone must be in there. I could see a shadow on the floor by the bed. Someone was sitting on my bed. Walter had come back after all! I put the tray down on the floor of the passage and rushed in.

But it wasn't Walter. It was Will. He was sitting cross-legged on my bed and he was reading Walter's letter. Humph was on the bed beside him.

'Well, little sister,' he said, waving it at me. 'What have you been up to, then? And who is this W.R. who wrote this letter?' I'd forgotten to hide it away. What a fool I'd been! What an idiot! He picked up the bottle and opened it. 'Smells of mint,' he said. 'And it's one of my bottles from my lab. So it *was* you messing about down there, wasn't it?' I said nothing because there was nothing I could say. 'I thought so. But why, that's what I want to know? You've never showed any interest in chemistry before, have you? Something's going on here, Bessy, and you'd better tell me, else I'll take these downstairs and show them and I don't think you'd want that, would you?'

'You've got no right to be in here,' I said. 'It's my room. I don't come in your room, do I?'

'I only came in to find out what Humph was up to,' he said. 'I saw him whining and scratching at your door. Thought that was a bit funny. So I opened the door and let him in. He came straight to your table and started sniffing at this letter. Don't suppose I'd have noticed it otherwise. Now what's it all about? You can tell me. You can trust me. I promise I won't tell. Cross my heart I won't.'

'You wouldn't believe me anyway,' I said. 'You'd just think I was telling stories. You always think I'm telling stories.' I was playing for time. I had run out of ideas. I'd promised Walter I wouldn't tell anyone about him. He'd kept his side of the bargain and I'd keep mine. He was my secret friend, and like he'd said they'd think I was mad if I told them about him – and it could finish Gran off for good if she ever found that there was a ghost living with us in the house.

Luckily, Humph chose this moment to take matters into his own hands (or paws, I suppose). He sprang off the bed and made for the open door and Gran's breakfast tray outside in the passage. He had his nose in the toast before I could stop him. I ran after him and shouted to him to get off, which he did, but so clumsily that he blundered all over the breakfast tray sending everything scattering and crashing in all directions; and as I lunged for him he fled, tail between his legs, with a piece of toast still in his mouth. He met Mother and Father coming up the stairs.

'What the dickens is going on up there?' Mother said as the tea ran across the floorboards and began to trickle down the stairs towards her. As you can imagine I was in a very difficult position. To blame Will would have been like waving a red rag to a bull – he would have been bound to tell them everything there and then, just out of spite. So I blamed Humph instead.

'It was Humph,' I said, starting to pick myself up. 'He ran right into me. Knocked me over. I couldn't help it. Honest.' I peeled a piece of toast off my elbow.

'You all right, dear?' said Mother running up the stairs with Father close behind. 'I've said time and again that dog should be shut out the back.' She was helping me up. 'It's dangerous for Gran. She's always tripping over him. And he licks Little Jim like he's a lollipop. It's not healthy, and he's always the wrong side of every door. He should stay outside.'

'What's the matter?' It was Gran calling from her room. 'What's going on out there?'

'Nothing, dear,' said Mother. 'A little accident that's all. No one's hurt. Don't you worry, we'll bring you your breakfast in a minute.' Will had said nothing so far, and I thought the danger was over. But then he saw his milk jug. It was the milk jug that made him do it – he told me as much later on.

Miraculously it was the only thing that was broken, but unfortunately for me it was the milk jug Will made in pottery class at school and he'd given it to Mother for her birthday only a few weeks before. He was very, very proud of it.

There were tears in his eyes as he bent down and picked up the pieces. He looked up at me and I knew right away what he was going to do. 'Got something to show you, Father,' he said. 'In Bessy's room. Come and look.' And he got up and went into my room. Mother and Father followed him. I couldn't stop him now. 'Look,' I heard him say. 'There's this letter and this. . . .' I dared not go in. I didn't want to look.

'What letter?' said Father. 'What are you rabbiting on about?'

'But it *was* here, Father,' said Will, a rising panic in his voice. 'On the bed it was. Honest. And there was this little bottle too and it was full of green stuff.' My heart rose. I understood at once what had happened, and I knew instinctively who had come to my rescue.

'What bottle?' I asked innocently as I went into my bedroom. Will was on all fours looking under the bed.

'It *was* here! I know it was!'

'Getting as bad as your sister, Will,' said Father looking around the room. 'Lives in a world of her own, don't you Bessy? Always telling stories and making things up. Not like you to be fanciful, Will. Can't see any bottle, can you, dear?'

'All I can see,' said Mother, 'is that you haven't made your bed yet, Bess. You promised me you'd keep your room tidier. You know I haven't got time to clear up after you, not now, not with Little Jim to look after. I'll tidy up that mess outside, if you tidy up in here.' And she went over to open the window. 'Smells of Humph in here, and tobacco smoke,' she said sniffing the curtains. 'You haven't been smoking, have you Bess?' I shook my head.

'It's Will that has a fag on the sly from time to time,' said Father, 'isn't it Will?' And he put his arm around Will's shoulder. Will opened his mouth to deny it but didn't even bother. No one would believe him and he knew it. 'Still, no great harm in that,' Father went on. 'We all have one or two when we're young just to try it. But best not to do it up here, Will. Not safe to smoke in bedrooms.'

'Don't you go encouraging him,' said Mother. 'It's not safe to smoke anywhere. It's a horrible habit and it kills you.' And then Little Jim began crying downstairs and she ran out. Will kept looking over his shoulder at me as he left the room. He was as much bewildered as angry I think, though I know he'd have cheerfully killed me at that moment given half a chance. They were gone at last and I was alone in my room.

I coughed loudly four times and my friend Walter appeared. He was leaning on the mantelpiece, the remains of a smile on his lips. He threw back his cloak. The letter was tucked in his belt and he had the bottle in his hand. 'One day that dog of yours will be the cause of our undoing, Bess,' he said with a laugh, and he puffed purposefully on his pipe. I put my finger to my lips for fear we would be overheard.

'Where were you last night?' I whispered. 'I called you and called you.'

'Your grandmother is well again I trust?' he asked. I nodded. 'I'm glad of it.' He held up the bottle. 'The elixir I discovered whilst I was a prisoner in the Tower. It took years of work to perfect it. They allowed me to use a shed underneath the wall for my experiments. There is something to be said for imprisonment. It is a life without distraction and concentrates the mind most wonderfully. I administered this medicine to my friends and family, even to my jailors, and they were glad of it.'

'Why didn't you come last night?' I asked. 'I only wanted to say sorry. I didn't really mean all those things I said, and I wanted to thank you for saving Gran like you did.'

'Sweet cousin,' he said, putting his hands on my shoulders and kissing me on the forehead. 'I cannot in truth be thanked for restoring to health one whom I myself brought so nearly to the point of death. You see before you a miserable fellow whose life was wasted in many fruitless schemes. They came to nothing and through mine own vanity too. In truth, I had hoped in my spirit life to improve myself, to mend my ways. But I see now my character is quite unredeemable. You were right indeed to scold me as you did, and you should not thank me now, cousin. I have repaired the damage I myself have caused, and even in so doing I have placed you again under threat of discovery. I had not thought to destroy the letter and the elixir. I had not thought they might be discovered nor even how you would explain it if they were. I am an old fool, cousin. I am a blundering, vain old fool, the same as I ever was. Blame not your brother, dear Bess, for he is much perplexed by what has passed. In truth I see in him something of myself as a boy – quick to temper and quick to tears, but he has a kind heart and will grow to a fine man.'

'He's a pig,' I said. 'Wasn't my fault his jug broke. It was Humph. And he goes and tells everyone like that. Serves him right.'

'The dog again,' said Sir Walter. 'That miserable cur follows me everywhere, even though I do not feed him any more. I had not thought a spirit has enough scent about him for a dog to follow.'

'Probably the tobacco,' I said. 'I told you not to smoke in the house, and you said you wouldn't.'

'Indeed I did, cousin, and truly I meant to keep my word.' Walter took the pipe out of his mouth and looked at it ruefully. 'But I do it without thinking. 'Tis a habit of three hundred years or more, chick, and not easy to break. For certain it can no longer do me much harm.' And he chuckled.

'Last night I thought you had gone for ever,' I said. 'Where did you go?'

'To the river, for I had much to think on and it is a fine

place to do it,' he said; and then he looked at me long and hard. 'I fear I must leave you, cousin. Whether it be the dog, the smell of tobacco or your brother Will, were I to stay here there can be little doubt that one day we will be discovered and that might prove grave indeed for your grandmother. I mean not to play on words, but it is apt enough. You know that I have come close to killing her once already. To stay would risk only a greater disaster. I shall meddle no more, sweet cousin. I had meant to stay and do you and your family some service if I could, but I may not risk another day here. I must be gone from this place before it is too late.'

'No!' I protested and too loudly.

Walter held his finger to his lips. 'It must be so, chick. If I go now, our secret is safe and no harm is done. I have tasted again the sweet air of my youth and I have found such a friend in you, dear Bess, that I do not wish to leave your side nor ever to leave this place; but it needs must be. It is not safe to stay, and besides, I have matters at home that call me back.'

'Home?' I said. 'What home?'

'Why, the Tower, cousin. I delude myself if I think otherwise. The Tower is my home. I have none other.'

'Am I ever going to see you again?' I asked, fighting to hold back my tears.

'You know where you can find me,' he said, 'if ever you have need of me. You have but to come and I shall be there.' I turned away from him and wiped my eyes. 'You should be brave. It is I that should weep for it is I that must go. You have much to rejoice in here – a fine father and a loving mother, and a brother who also loves you, but who knows not yet how to say it or to show it. Little Jim loves only his food, but I would wager you will be the apple of his eye as the years pass.' He took my chin in his hand and lifted it. 'But I warn you, dear cousin. There are storms ahead. You will have need of all your courage. So no more tears.'

'Storms?' I asked. He was speaking in riddles as he often did. 'What do you mean?'

'I fear you will understand and that soon enough, but I can say no more. I shall meddle no more in your affairs. I will be with you but in spirit only. I would fain stay with you, cousin, and protect you from all that lies ahead of you, but I may not. I belong no more to your world. I had plans afoot to help you – indeed they were already much advanced, but I see now that I have always been the cause of more harm in this world than good, however noble my intentions – and I confess they were not always so. You may fare better without me, cousin, than with me; if you only remember that storms always pass by and give way to clear blue skies. Mark me well and remember these words. Only have faith that all will be well and it shall be so. Only believe a thing is and it is. Believe it is not and it is not. Count on it, sweet cousin, for it is true. We must bear all, and bravely too.' He stepped back from me and wiped the tears from my cheeks with his cloak.

'I must be gone, back to London; but I do not think I should take the horse again. It is commonly thought that ghosts can fly but they cannot, and so neither can I. How else then may I come to London?'

'Father's going in to town in the car and I can take you on to the station,' I said. I did not try to change his mind because I could see it was already quite made up. It was no problem to find a good excuse to go with Father into Exeter that afternoon – I needed to change some library books.

It was a sombre journey. Father was very preoccupied, and hardly said a word to me all the way. He wasn't concentrating much on his driving either. More than once we nearly ran into the car in front, and he even lost his way in the city centre. I prattled on as best I could about Gran and Sally but I could tell that he wasn't really listening to me. Walter sat in the back seat all the way looking out of the window and when we got to town Father dropped us off outside the library. He had to go to the bank, he said, and he'd be back in an hour and a half. I was to wait on the steps of the library for him.

We walked in silence through the streets of Exeter, Walter and I, down towards the station. When we got there they said a train was due in a quarter of an hour. No one ever looks at the tickets at the barrier – not that we needed one. When the train came in I opened the door of a first-class carriage. Sir Walter Raleigh ought at least to travel first-class, I thought. I looked over my shoulder before I spoke. There were only a few people on the platform and they were all busy. I could talk without fear of being overheard. 'How will you know your way in London?' I asked.

'I have travelled often on the Underground,' Walter said. 'Though I do not like the press of people about me it is a convenient way to get about. It is unnatural I think for a man to travel like a mole but I am accustomed to it now. Fear not, cousin. Tonight I shall rest in my bed in the Tower.' Doors slammed to the right and the left and someone bellowed for me to stand clear. 'Farewell sweet cousin,' said my friend Walter leaning out of the window, and he lifted my hand and kissed it. 'Think kindly of me, and often, I pray you.'

I could not bring my voice to say anything, but I waved and blew kisses until the train had vanished and my friend Walter with it.

'You all right?' It was a railway guard, and he was frowning down at me, his cap on the back of his head. 'I been watching you. First you walks along the platform and opens the door of the train. Then you closes it and then you talks like you was saying goodbye to someone. And then you waves goodbye and now there's tears all over your face. It's like you was saying goodbye to no one. You sure you're all right?' I nodded and walked away fast towards the stairs. 'You on your own, are you? Where's your mum?' he called after me. 'Where's your dad?'

I began to run. I think I ran all the way back to the

library without stopping. I had a terrible urge inside me to catch the next train to London and follow him to the Tower. I had lost my friend and I was going to be alone again. I didn't know if I was more sorry for him or more sorry for me. Either way I was miserable.

I was sitting waiting on the steps of the library for Father when I had an idea. If I couldn't have Walter with me then I would have the next best thing. I would find a book about him from the library and read it. That way I could find out more about him and I could get to know him better even if he wasn't there. The book I found had very small print and only one picture of him, on the title page. It was of Walter Raleigh as a young man, but I recognised the way he stood leaning on his cane, a half-smile on his lips, his legs crossed.

I was half way through the first page when Father drew up. I could see at once that something was wrong. He was grey and drawn and he said not a single word all the way home. I asked him what the matter was, whether he was feeling ill, but he didn't even reply. It was as if he had never heard me. I had to wait until we got home to find out what had happened.

He walked around the garden with his arm around Mother and then out into Front Meadow beyond. With Will beside me I watched and waited for them to come back. When they did I could see that Mother had been crying, but she tried not to show it. 'I've got some bad news,' Father said, 'and your mother says I ought to tell you. Well, here goes. We've got to leave the farm. We've got to sell up.'

'What do you mean?' said Will. 'What do you mean, sell up?'

'Nothing else for it.' said Father. 'We can't pay the rent on the place and so we've got to go. I've just been in to see the bank manager. He says we can't go on, not any more. That's all there is to it.'

# CHAPTER 6

IT TOOK SOME TIME FOR IT TO SINK IN. WE SAT together, the four of us, in the hay barn. We could talk there, Mother said, without any danger of Gran overhearing. Beside me Father was sitting forward with his elbows on his knees picking the nail of his forefinger with his thumb nail. It was left to Mother to explain it all. To be honest it didn't much matter to me why it happened. I mean it didn't make any difference, did it? We were selling the farm and that was all there was to it. I suppose Mother was doing her best to make it hurt less.

'We've done all we can,' she said. 'Your father's worked himself to the bone. But it was always an uphill struggle on this land. It never was the best farm in the world but we knew that when we took it on, didn't we dear?' Father stared straight ahead of him and said nothing. Mother went on.

'The land's steep and a lot of it faces north, and it's wet land, too. Still, we've managed to make ends meet over the years. But we've had a bit of bad luck just these last two or three years – poor lambing for the last couple of years, a lot of singles and then we had that scour. The price of pigs has fallen and you remember there was that blight in the potatoes last year. We hardly lifted any good ones at all. We were hoping for a good corn harvest this year, but it wasn't good enough. The sums just weren't adding up and that's what farming's all about in the end. The sums have got to add up. 'Course, if we owned the farm we could sell of a bit of land and we'd be all right again then, but we don't. As you know, it belongs to Mr Watts.'

'I don't like Mr Watts,' said Will.

'Like him or not, Will, he's the landlord,' said Mother, 'and we've got to pay him his rent. We've had to borrow money from the bank to pay the rent for three years now and Father says they won't let us do it again. So there's nothing else for it. Only way to pay the bank back is to sell up, but we'll need to sell everything.'

'Not everything,' said Will.

'Everything,' Father snapped, standing up suddenly. 'Cows, sheep, bullocks, machinery. And Sally, she'll have to go too.'

'But how are we going to farm without any animals, without any tractors?' I asked.

'We aren't going to farm,' said Father. 'Not any more.'

'Well anyway, we've still got the house, haven't we?' said Will.

Father turned on us. 'Don't you understand, Will? We've got to go. We've got to leave the house as well. It belongs to the landlord, to Mr Watts, same as the farm does. If we can't pay the rent, and we can't, he'll want us out. We're six months overdue with the rent already and the bank won't let us have any more money. *Now* do you understand?'

'You mean we can't even live here any more?' I said, and as I said it I understood at last the whole terrible truth. So that had been the reason for Father's black moods, for his long, deep silences of recent weeks. That was why Mother and Father were shouting at each other in the kitchen that evening. 'We mustn't say a word about it to Gran,' said Mother. 'She mustn't know yet, not until she's completely better. We've somehow got to tell her so it doesn't upset her too much.'

'But where are we going to live?' said Will, his eyes full of tears. 'Where are we going to go? We've always lived here.'

'Over twenty years I've farmed this land, Will,' said Father. 'We'll just have to find somewhere else, that's all.'

'Another farm?' said Will brightening a bit.

Father shook his head. 'You need money to run a farm and I'm not borrowing it. What we make on the sale of the animals and machinery will just about pay off the bank. I'm never borrowing another penny, not as long as I live.'

'I told Aunty Ellie this might happen,' said Mother, 'and she said right away we could go and live with her, just till we've sorted things out a bit. She's got plenty of room. Perhaps it'll be a blessing after all. You never can tell. As Gran says, "every cloud has a silver lining".'

'I know,' said Will who was beginning to cry openly now. 'And there's a light at the end of every tunnel.' And he rushed out of the hay barn. Father went after him.

'I think your father's more upset for Will than he is for himself,' said Mother standing up and brushing the hay off her skirt.

'How long before we've got to go?' I asked.

'The solicitor says we've got to be out by Michaelmas, and that's less than two months away. There'll be a lot to do, Bessie dear, and perhaps that's just as well. Come on, young lady.' And she took my hand and we went outside into the sunlight.

'What will Father do?' I asked.

'He'll find a job somewhere, I suppose,' said Mother.

'What if he can't?'

'Then I'll find a job,' said Mother.

'But what if you can't find a job?'

'What if? What if?' Mother said. 'We'll manage, you'll see. We always have, haven't we? Let's just ride out this storm Bess, before we face the next one.'

Hadn't someone else talked to me of storms ahead? Is this what Walter had meant? Is this what he was warning me about? But how could he possibly have known this was going to happen? Why did he have to talk in riddles?

'Not a word to Gran now, remember?' was the last thing Mother said to me before we went back into the house.

Within a day or two Gran was sent off to stay with Aunty Ellie. It would be better that way and safer, Mother said. Aunty Ellie would tell her gently, when she felt the time was right.

At school it soon got around that the Throckmortons were being put off the farm and everyone wanted to know where we were going and why. In the playground after lunch one day Will had a fight with Simon Battle – it *would* be him, he picked fights with everyone. Simon Battle told Will that he'd heard Father had been drinking too much in the evenings at 'The Mucky Duck' (it was really The Black Swan, but everyone called it 'The Mucky Duck') when he should have been out farming, and that was why we were having to leave the farm. Will didn't care too much for that and said so with his fists, leaving Simon Battle a bit bruised and battered. I was proud of my brother that day. Don't get me wrong, I don't like fighting, not normally.

But in some ways life changed for the better, strange as that may seem. Everyone, except Simon Battle and one or two others, felt sorry for us. The teachers were all as sweet as pie, so that Will got away with blue murder; and my pictures and poems were always put on the wall in the classroom – I even had one up in the front hall. They were all good of course, but not that good. But this was small enough compensation for the misery facing us every afternoon when we got back home from school.

You couldn't call it home, not any more. The farm was full of strange people wandering around scrutinizing the cows and looking into the sheep's mouths. They inspected the machinery and clambered all over the barn. They peered down the drains and wells, and sniffed at the hay. And they weren't only out on the farm. They were in the house as well. I came back from school one day and found a man in a Sherlock Holmes hat up in my bedroom pushing his penknife into the window-sill. 'Just testing for dry rot,' he said. 'Lots of it about in this house. No central heating, I see. Nothing much been done in this place for a few years, by the look of it.' I felt like knocking his silly hat off. I never discovered who he was. I never knew who any of them were, except Mr Watts.

I recognised Mr Watts, the landlord. You could hardly miss him. He had a face so purple and puffed up that I thought he might blow up one day and fly away snorting like a balloon. Of course I'd seen him out on the farm with Father from time to time. He used to come around a couple of times a year to inspect the farm gates and the ditches and the hedges. In spite of everything, Father and he still seemed very friendly and I could not understand that at all. After all, this was the man who was kicking us out of our home, and kicking Father off his farm. Well, I wasn't going to smile at him nor have him give me one of his horrible humbugs he was always offering me. Will disliked him just as much, but the trouble was he loved humbugs, so he took all the humbugs he was offered; but at least he never smiled at Mr Watts and he never said thank you.

It was at nights that I thought most about my friend Walter alone in his cold, damp room up in the Tower of London and I longed to have him with me again. Every night I read the book about him that I'd brought back from the library. There were a lot of long words I didn't understand, but I understood enough to know that everything he'd told me was true. Walter Raleigh was never a traitor. They *had* taken everything away from him and they hadn't even given him a fair trial. I could quite understand why he wanted revenge.

I was angry at him, though, angry that he had left me when I needed him most. True, he had warned me of the 'storms' ahead, and now I knew perfectly well what he had meant by that. But I wondered over and over again how he had known about what would happen; and if he had known, then why hadn't he stayed to help me? I remembered every night his words of hope to me just before he left and said them over and over to myself just before I went to sleep. I said them so often that I came to believe them absolutely.

'Storms always pass and give way to clear blue skies. Have faith that all will be well and it will be so. Only believe a thing is and it is, believe it is not and it is not.' If my friend Walter said everything would be all right, then it would be. I never doubted it. And because of that I can honestly say that those last few weeks at the farm were the happiest I can remember. I knew for sure that something would happen, perhaps at the last moment so that somehow we would be able to stay on at the farm. That's what I told Will, too. Of course he wanted to believe me, and I think in the end he did. He must have done, because we certainly did not mope, either of us.

Every daylight hour when we weren't in school we'd be out together on the farm, the two of us, no matter what the weather. It was as if Will wanted to make the most of every day (just in case the worst came to the worst, perhaps) and for some reason he wanted me to be with him all the time. And I liked that. Maybe it was because Father was so busy getting ready for the sale and packing up. Maybe he just didn't want to be on his own, I don't know and I don't care. Whatever the reason, Will turned into a proper brother during those weeks – or did I turn into a proper sister? Either way we scarcely ever quarrelled, though he did ask me time and again about the letter and the bottle he had found in my bedroom, each time probing deeper and deeper. I just told him it was a secret and I couldn't tell him, not yet, but that one day soon I would tell him everything. Each day he wondered if that day had come and I had to put him off. We became such good friends that I was often tempted to tell him all about my friend Walter, but I didn't like breaking promises and I still wasn't sure whether Will would believe me.

We went fishing together almost every day if the river wasn't too high and he'd let me use his rod whenever I wanted. He taught me how to make a fly and how to tie it so it didn't keep coming off and what flies to use in what weather and where the fish lie. We rode out on Sally, both of us up, with me behind clinging on. We picked every blackberry on the farm that wasn't too green or too squashy to eat. We ate most of them ourselves and gave the rest to Sally and the pigs, and we came home black-mouthed and blue-lipped. We stripped the apple trees and went mushrooming every morning before breakfast. 'Not going to leave a thing for the next people,' Will said. 'Saw the horrible Barrowbills looking over the farm this afternoon. Couldn't bear it if they moved in here.'

'There won't be any next people,' I said. 'We'll still be here. You'll see.'

'I hope you're right,' he said. 'The sale's less than a week away now, five days.' My faith in Walter's words was becoming a little fragile now, so I prayed each night too, just for good measure.

By the morning of the sale I think I knew it was almost

hopeless to go on believing that anything could stop it now, but I clung to the little faith I had left. You never know, I told myself. You never know. The whole farm had been invaded by lorries and Landrovers and laughing farmers leaning on sticks, and it was difficult for Will and me to get away and be on our own. In the end we found the haystack was the only place. I was sitting next to Will, high up in the haystack, looking down the yard where the auctioneers had set up a temporary sale ring.

When the hammer fell for the first time and Celandine the Twelfth, Father's favourite cow, was sold, I understood at last the emptiness of Walter Raleigh's comforting words. They had been false words. Everything he had said had sounded so good, so believable. I saw Mother and Father standing beside the auctioneer, and the fixed sadness on their faces brought tears of anger to my eyes. One by one the cows were driven in and sold, and after them the sheep and then the pigs. Everything was going. It was too late now. There was no hope left. My friend Walter had betrayed me. He had lied to me and I would tell him so.

'I'm going fishing,' I said.

'All right, I'll see you down there,' said Will, who had not taken his eyes off the ring below. 'I'll just wait to see Sally sold. I want to know who she goes to. I just hope those horrible Barrowbills don't get her, that's all. They've bought almost all the pigs, y'know.'

I began to climb down the haystack. 'Bessy,' Will called after me. I stopped and looked up at him. 'You told me it would never happen,' he said. 'And it is happening, isn't it?' I couldn't say anything. There was nothing to say. 'It's not your fault, I suppose,' he said. 'Not anyone's fault.'

I left him sitting there. No one saw me as I went into the house and up into my room to fetch my things. As I crept past Little Jim's room I could hear Aunty Ellie singing to him while she changed his nappy. The tune was 'Three Blind Mice'. 'Mucky pup, mucky pup,' she sang. 'Who's a mucky pup? Who's a mucky pup?' Lucky Little Jim, I thought: he doesn't know what's going on. He'll never even remember today. I emptied my piggy bank. If I included the ten pounds I got from Aunty Ellie last Christmas I had almost twenty pounds in all – just about enough to get me to London, and back, I thought.

It was quite easy to get to Exeter. I got a lift in one of the cattle trucks that had just finished loading in the farm lane. I told the driver some cock-and-bull story about visiting my gran in hospital. He seemed to believe me and so that's where he dropped me. It was a long walk from there down to the station, but I wasn't worried. I knew there were trains to London often enough.

'Be along in ten minutes,' said the man in the ticket office. 'Do you want a return?'

'Yes.'

'On your own are you?' He examined me keenly through the glass. 'A bit young to be on your own, aren't you?'

'I'm thirteen,' I lied keeping my eyes down as I counted out my money.

'You don't look it,' he said.

'Well I am,' I said. I felt he was still suspicious after he gave me the ticket, so I walked as tall as I could and as quickly as I could through the ticket barrier towards the train.

The train was crowded but I managed to find a seat next to a lady with silver-white hair who smelt of cough sweets. Opposite me was an old man who slept almost all the way to London with his mouth open. I was so fascinated by the repeated attempts of a large fly to look inside his mouth that the journey passed quickly enough.

I had been on the Underground twice before but never on my own, and so I was soon lost. The Underground map was a multi-coloured maze to me, so I gave up and tried to ask someone. But there were so many people and they all seemed in such a hurry to get wherever it was they were going to that it was difficult to stop anyone and ask them. In the end I managed to ask a Chinese lady who didn't speak English very well but she knew where Tower Hill Station was and pointed back in the direction I'd just come from. She even came with me to be sure I got on the right train.

So I found myself at last, late that afternoon, walking past the guards and the Beefeaters, past Traitors' Gate and up the hill towards Tower Green and the Bloody Tower. Most people seemed to be coming out already and there were no queues outside the Crown Jewels or the Bloody Tower. On Tower Green three ravens fought noisily over the remains of a pork pie, and a Beefeater posed for a photograph surrounded by a party of raucous children. I took the steps up to the Bloody Tower in twos hoping to find myself alone. I had prepared exactly what I would say to him. I wasn't going to mince words, I can tell you. He shouldn't have told me everything will work out just because you think it will. I'd tell him just what I thought of him.

His room was packed with people on a guided tour. I did not recognise the language they were speaking – it wasn't French, I knew that much – all I know is that the guide loved to talk. He spent ten minutes rambling on and on, and it all ended when he gave himself a mock chop on the back of the head, and everyone roared with laughter. They took a few photographs and then they were gone and I was alone. I coughed four times. Nothing. I tried again, louder this time. Nothing. I whispered 'Walter! Walter! Where are you?' Still nothing.

I made for Raleigh's Walk. At the far end there were a few people leaning out over the wall and calling out to friends below. But they were some way away and so I coughed anyway, loudly and deliberately four times. They turned and looked at me rather sharply, almost suspiciously; and so I got out my handkerchief and continued my coughing fit, just to convince them.

'I hear you, cousin. I hear you, cousin.' I turned around. My friend Walter was standing by the doorway, his black cloak wrapped around him; and he walked towards me now, his arms outstretched to greet me.

# CHAPTER 7

ALL THE ANGER INSIDE ME EVAPORATED AS HE embraced me and then, putting his cloak around me, he led me back through the narrow doorway into his room. 'Dearest cousin,' he said, 'you cannot know what joy it brings me to see you again.' As he looked at me his brow furrowed suddenly into a frown and the smile left his lips. 'Yet I dread to know why you have come. There is something in your eyes that tells me it is not just to see your friend Walter. Is it bad tidings that you bring me, cousin? Your grandmother?'

I shook my head. 'She's all right,' I said.

'Then it needs must be the farm,' said Walter. 'Has it happened so soon? My poor Bess, have they taken the farm from you, and your home too? I see from your face that I have hit the mark.'

'How did you know?' I asked.

'It is in the nature of the spirit, cousin,' he said, 'to be a spy, to eavesdrop. Many a time I sat with your mother and father in the kitchen as they tried to find a way out. I saw the papers, cousin, I read the letters from the bank and from the landlord. I thought this might happen in the end – your mother thought so too – but your father is a fighter and I thought matters might yet be put right. I hoped as he did that a good harvest might save him. Is there no hope at all?'

'The sale's today,' I said. 'We've had to sell everything, even Sally.' My friend Walter shook his head sadly and looked away. 'We're moving out tomorrow,' I went on. 'We're going to live at Aunty Ellie's till we can find somewhere else.' And he put his arms out and hugged me to him. 'You said it would be all right,' I cried, burying my face in his cloak. 'You said that if I believed it enough then everything would turn out all right, and I did believe it like you said but nothing turned out right.'

I felt him stiffen. Then his hands were on my shoulders and pushing me away from him. When I looked up, his face was smiling and his eyes shining with excitement. 'And so it shall be, chick. So it shall. I will meddle just once more in your world but to better effect this time, I trust. I had a mind to do this before but I did not dare to for fear of blundering. But now I see I have no choice.' He wiped my eyes with his cloak. 'Be sure dear cousin, that all that can be done will be done to restore your family's fortune, and mine too.'

'But it's too late,' I said. 'I told you the sale's today. It'll be over by now.'

'It is never too late,' Walter replied, turning to go. 'But we must make haste. I may not be able to restore your home and your farm, but I have something else in mind that will do almost as well; and in doing it I may kill two birds with one stone. I pray you, cousin, bide here a few minutes for there is something that must be done before we leave.' He laughed aloud, a triumphant, almost a vengeful laugh. 'I have thought of it often, but never before had just cause or purpose. Now I have. Fortune may be fickle but she can sometimes be sweet. Stay where you are, cousin, and I will return.' And he was gone.

I did not have long to wait. The tourists I had seen out on Raleigh's Walk passed back through the room. They looked at me somewhat strangely, whispering to each other. It occurred to me then that they might have witnessed my sudden disappearance under Walter's cloak, and I smiled at the thought of what they must have seen. One of them looked as if they were going to talk to me so I turned away and pretended to be engrossed in the view from the window. When I turned around a few minutes later they were gone and my friend Walter was back, a wicked twinkle in his eye. 'We should not tarry here one moment longer, cousin,' he said. 'I have taken the honey from the hive – the honeycomb itself – and would have thee far from here before it is discovered. I fear it may make them mad.'

'Who?'

'Why, the bees, dear cousin,' he said with a chuckle. He was talking in riddles again.

'What honey? What bees?' I asked.

'All in good time, dearest Bess. I promise you shall know all I have done and all I intend to do. But this is not the time for explanations. All will be well. Just believe it and all will be well.'

'You said that once before,' I said.

'Indeed I did, cousin Bess, but sometimes faith needs a little encouragement, and belief a helping hand. But no more of this. We must be gone. Lead on, chick, and I shall follow. Make haste and be sure that I shall be with you all the way back to Devon, whether you see me or not.'

The ravens were still squabbling over the last of the pork pie on Tower Green as we came down the steps of the Bloody Tower. A Beefeater was removing an upturned ice-cream cone from the railings where someone had stuck it. He was muttering to himself as we passed. 'Mucky pups,' he said. 'Mucky pups.'

And that set me thinking about Little Jim at home, and how they would all be worried sick about me. I should have left a note or something. I should have told Will. I should have told someone. I just never thought of it. It was already the worst day of their lives and I had to go and make it worse. And for what? For a trip up to London to shout at my friend Walter about how he'd let me down. And I hadn't even shouted at him, and he wasn't going to let me down. He had something up his sleeve – that was all I knew; but I had no idea what it was, and there was no time to ask him, not now. What was I going to say to them when I got back? 'Sorry Mother, sorry Father, sorry Will. I didn't mean to upset you but I've got this ghost friend I went to see. He's sitting here right beside me, and he says everything will be all right. He's come home to help us, but I don't know how.' It didn't sound very convincing. No, I could tell them nothing, only that I was sorry to have worried them and that I was coming home.

I found the telephones on Paddington Station. Most of them didn't work, but I found one that did and put in my money. The telephone rang. Father answered. 'Cripes, Bess, where the dickens have you been? You all right? Where are you?'

'Paddington Station.'

'Paddington?'

'I'm catching the next train home, Father,' I said. I could hear him shouting to Mother that I was all right. She came to the telephone, her voice heavy with crying. 'I'm sorry, Mother,' I said. 'I didn't mean to. I was upset. I just ran away. I had to.'

'Doesn't matter, dear,' she said. 'All that matters is that

you're safe, and you're coming home. We'll meet you at the station. You frightened the life out of us, Bess.' And then she began to laugh. I could hear Humph barking in the background. I could see it all – Will jumping up and down, and Humph bounding around him in his excitement. The pips went on the phone and we were cut off.

I coughed as soon as I found an empty part of the carriage to be sure Walter was still there, and there he was sitting beside me in the window seat swamped in his black cloak. 'I fear you have very little faith in me, cousin,' he whispered. 'Have I not promised I will not leave your side?' And he lit up his pipe and sat back in his seat. When I looked again he wasn't there; but he was, if you know what I mean.

Of course no one else could see the smoke, but they could smell it all right. And they did. I wasn't to know that I had chosen a No Smoking seat, was I? I hadn't even thought to look. At the first stop – Reading, it was – a lady got in and sat down opposite us. She kept coughing and wiping her eyes and eyeing me angrily. So I held my nose and shrugged my shoulders. It wasn't long before she got up and moved away and we had the whole carriage to ourselves. Then the ticket collector came round. He must have been about seven foot tall. He sniffed the air deliberately. 'Are you on your own?' he asked, taking my ticket. I nodded. 'Someone meeting you at the other end, are they?'

'Yes,' I said.

'That's all right then,' said the ticket collector sniffing again. 'Bit of a pong in here. I've had a complaint. Lady back there says you been smoking. You been smoking, have you?' I shook my head. He handed me back my ticket. 'Bad for you, you know. Stunts your growth. Never had one in my life.' And he was gone.

It was dark by the time we got back to Exeter. They were all there waiting on the platform: Mother, Father, Will and Little Jim. Mother and Father hugged me so I could hardly breathe and I think they cried a bit, even Father. Little Jim grabbed my nose and pulled it which made me screech – he had such sharp little nails. Will was the only one who didn't seem at all pleased to see me. He just looked at me coldly; and I could see that Father, although he was relieved to have me back, was angry under it all and trying hard not to show it.

'Everyone's been out looking for you,' he said as we walked back along the platform. 'What were you thinking of, going off like that?'

'I told you, dear,' said Mother, 'she was upset, weren't you Bess?' I nodded.

'I thought so,' Mother went on. 'She just couldn't take any more, could you dear? I mean there was times today when I would have done the same thing myself given half a chance. We didn't even know you were missing till after the sale, teatime it was.'

'To go running off like that without so much as . . .' Father was getting into his stride but Mother looked at him and stopped him before he got going.

'Never mind all that, dear,' she said firmly. 'There's no real harm done, not now she's back.'

'But she's got to know the trouble she's caused,' Father insisted. 'I mean, we had the police out looking along the river bank. They put frogmen in the river. Will said you told him you were going fishing. We thought you'd fallen in and drowned.'

'Sorry,' I said. 'I didn't mean it, honest I didn't. It was all those people and then Sally was going to be sold and I just wanted to get away, that's all.'

'We understand, dear,' said Mother.

'I'm not so sure *they* will,' said Father, nodding towards the ticket barrier.

Two policemen were standing there; I recognised one of them as the same one who had come when Sally went missing. They were both looking hard at me as I came towards them. Neither looked very pleased to see me. 'And where have you been, young lady?' said the one with the peaked cap, the one I'd seen before.

'London,' I said.

'You've put a lot of people to a lot of trouble, you know that?' I nodded and looked down at my feet because I didn't want to look him in the eye. 'I don't know why you went, but don't you ever go off like that again, do you hear me? Promise me, now.'

'Promise,' I said, and I meant it.

'I'll call off the search then, Mr Throckmorton.'

'Thanks,' said Father shaking his hand, 'and I'm sorry we've put you to so much trouble.'

'It's what we're here for,' he said. 'All's well that ends well, eh?' He'd borrowed another of Gran's favourite sayings.

Will never said a word to me, not in the station and not in the Landrover all the way home. But I sensed he was looking at me in the darkness and it made me feel uncomfortable. I coughed four times and with some relief I saw the dark shape of Walter appear beside him.

We were back home in the kitchen before Will said a word to me. Mother had taken Little Jim up to bed and Father was taking Humph out for his walk as he always did last thing at night. At first there was a silence between us. 'Why didn't you tell me?' Will said suddenly. 'I wouldn't have said anything.'

'I know,' I said.

'You didn't want me to come with you, did you?' Will went on. He was hurt more than angry.

'It wasn't that,' I said. 'I just wanted to be alone, that's all.'

'And I've been thinking,' he said.

'What about?'

'That you wouldn't hardly go off like that unless you had a

reason, and a good reason. It doesn't make sense.'

'I told you, I wanted to be alone.'

'You can be alone down by the river,' said Will. 'You don't need to go all the way to London to be alone, do you? There's something you're not telling me, Bess.' Mother came in at that moment and it was just as well. It was obvious that Will didn't believe a word I'd said.

'Little Jim's fast asleep,' Mother said. She put the kettle on the stove and sat down heavily. 'Well, there's a day I never want to have to live through again. Still, it's over now. All we've got to do is clear up this mess tomorrow and we'll be gone. I want to be out of here as quick as possible now.'

Humph scratched open the back door and came bounding in nose to the ground. He dashed straight through the kitchen, skidded in the hallway and thundered up the stairs. 'He'll wake up Little Jim,' said Mother.

'What's the matter with that dog?' said Father, putting the torch down on the kitchen table. 'Didn't seem to want his walk and that's not like him at all.' You could hear Humph shuffling along the passage upstairs. 'What the dickens is he after?' said Father, looking up at the ceiling.

'Dunno,' I said, but I knew all right. Will was looking at me and then up at the ceiling and then back at me. He was frowning. I knew for sure where my friend Walter was. There was no need for me to cough. The clock on the mantelpiece struck twelve.

'Weather forecast,' said Father. 'Always listen to the weather forecast last thing at night. Always have done. Not that it matters to me, now that I'm not a farmer any more.'

'You'll always be a farmer, dear,' Mother said going over to him and putting an arm round him. 'It's in your blood. Something will turn up, you'll see. We had a good sale, didn't we? Better than we could have hoped for. We'll be all right.'

The radio whistled and hissed until Father found the station he was looking for. '. . . *And here are the main headlines again tonight*.' I could hear Humph whining outside my room and scratching at the door. The voice on the radio faded in and out, but you could hear most of what was said: '*Police have confirmed tonight that one of the Crown Jewels is missing. One of the golden orbs, known as Queen Mary's Orb, has been stolen from the Tower of London. It is the first time that any of the Crown Jewels has been stolen. Police say that there is no evidence of a break-in and that no alarm was set off. Streets around the Tower are still sealed off tonight. A police spokesman said it was clearly the work of experts. The Crown Jewels, seen by millions of visitors each year, are kept under the tightest possible electronic security. The orb is said to be worth well over ten million pounds. And now here is the weather forecast . . .*'

I did not hear the weather forecast, for my head was swimming and the pounding of my heart was so loud in my ears that I thought everyone must hear it. The 'honeycomb'!

So that was the 'honeycomb' Walter was talking about in his riddle. It all fell into place in a few sickening seconds. Who else but a ghost, who else but my friend Walter, could steal the Crown Jewels without setting off alarms, without breaking anything? And who had disappeared for a few minutes and left me alone in the Bloody Tower? Who had talked of taking the 'honeycomb' and how angry the bees would be if it was discovered? My friend Walter had done it, and he was upstairs in my bedroom now; and six to one he had the golden orb from the Crown Jewels with him.

Mother put a mug of tea in front of me and stirred in the sugar. I felt as if I was being drawn down into it and would drown in the whirlpool of tea in front of my eyes. 'You all right, dear?' said Mother, pushing the hair back from my forehead to feel it. 'You're very pale all of a sudden and there's a cold sweat on you. Don't suppose you've had anything to eat all day, have you, dear?'

'No,' I said.

'Tired out I shouldn't wonder,' said Father switching off the radio. 'Well I'm blowed, did you hear that? How the devil did they manage it? We went up there once years ago. Coach trip, remember? You were there only a couple of months ago, weren't you, Bess? Went there with Aunty Ellie after that family gathering, didn't you?' I managed to nod. 'Don't know what they think they can do with it, though. Can hardly sell it, can they? I mean, someone would recognise it – most famous jewels in the world, they are. Still, ten million quid!' he whistled. 'What I couldn't do with a little of that just at the moment, and they say it pays to be honest. Ah well.' I dared not look across at Will for fear of catching his eye.

'Well, Bess went up to London today,' Will said, 'p 'raps she's brought it back with her.' And they all laughed at that. I tried to laugh with them but I think it came out more like a groan. We all went up to bed at the same time that night. At the top of the stairs Father kissed me on the forehead – just like my friend Walter – and I don't think he'd ever done that before. It was almost worth running away. 'Tomorrow can only be better,' he said.

Humph came lolloping out of my bedroom. 'Find what you were looking for, Humph?' said Father. 'Now get downstairs.' Humph looked up at him and went soulfully downstairs, stopping to look back over his shoulder every few steps as if there might be a reprieve. There wasn't. 'Tomorrow night we'll be at Aunty Ellie's and *she* won't let you sleep upstairs, that's for sure.' Humph sighed and went.

Will made as if to follow me into my room but Mother wouldn't let him. 'You can talk in the morning,' she said. 'Bess is tired out, and anyway the removal lorry will be here by seven o'clock. We've all got to be up early. Off to bed now.' And Will obeyed, a bit too easily I thought.

My room was not my room any more. All my owls had been packed away. There were no curtains at the windows, no pictures on the walls. 'Elephant' was nowhere to be seen. There was a packing case where my chair had been, and screwed-up newspaper was scattered around all over the floor. I shut the door and coughed. My friend Walter was sitting propped up against the pillows on my bed, his legs crossed at the ankles. He was smiling triumphantly. 'He knew I was here,' he said. 'That cur of yours sniffed me from head to toe and I had nothing to offer him, except this.' And he threw back his cloak. The golden orb lay on his lap shining and glittering in the light of my bedside lamp. I had guessed right, so it was no real surprise to me, but all the same I could not take my eyes off it. He held it out to me. 'It is yours, chick. Come, take it. It will not bite you.'

It was a perfect globe of gold encircled with bands of pearls and diamonds and rubies and sapphires and emeralds and many more stones that I could not recognise. At the top of it was a small, jewel-encrusted cross. I was about to touch it when I pulled back. 'You stole it, didn't you?' I said. 'You stole it from the Tower. It was on the radio. They're looking for it everywhere. You shouldn't have.'

'I am no thief, cousin,' Walter protested, his voice rising with indignation. 'Is it stealing to take what is mine? Did I not tell you how I was robbed of everything that was rightly mine, my lands, my castles, my jewels?' He held up the golden orb in one hand. 'This bauble is but a trifle of what I am owed, what is due to my family, to you. You are of my blood and therefore it is yours by right. Take it. I have only taken back what is ours, and ours it shall remain. I tell you, cousin I had more jewels on one of my shoes than there are in this trinket. Take it, for with it you can restore your family's fortune.'

'But it belongs to the Queen.'

'It belongs to you, Bess,' he said smiling, 'and if you will not take it then you must catch it.' And with that he tossed it to me. I had not time to think about dropping it, which was just as well because otherwise I would most certainly have done so. I can't catch to save my life. It was heavier than I expected, a lot heavier.

Suddenly the door behind me opened. I swung round, the golden orb in my hands. My brother Will was standing there, his mouth gaping.

'Cripes!' he said.

# CHAPTER 8

'YOU!' WILL SAID. 'IT WAS YOU! YOU STOLE IT. You really stole it.'

'No I didn't,' I said. He ignored me.

'But how? How did you do it?'

'I told you, I didn't do it. How could I? Close the door, Will, or they'll hear us.'

'I don't mind if they hear us.' He could not take his eyes off the orb. 'What did you do it for?'

'I never did it,' I whispered. 'Honest I didn't.'

'Then how come you're standing there holding it if you never took it?' He reached out and touched it. 'Is that really it?' he asked. 'Is that really the one?'

'I suppose so,' I said.

'Well, somebody stole it, didn't they?' I had nothing to

say. 'I mean it didn't get here on its own, did it, Bess? So if you didn't steal it, who did?'

'I can't tell you,' I said, 'not yet. And even if I could you wouldn't believe me. You'd just say I was making it all up.' Will looked at me for a moment and then suddenly he leaned forward and grabbed the orb out of my hands. 'If you won't tell me right now what's going on,' he said, 'I'll take this next door and show them. I will, Bess, honest I will. There's been things going on around here that I don't understand and you're going to tell me. For instance, I don't know how that letter and that bottle I found just disappeared. You said you'd tell me one day and you still haven't. One minute they were there and the next minute they weren't, and that's not natural. Then you go running off to London for no good reason, and now this. Something's going on, and I want to know what it is. Now are you going to tell me or not?'

'I would if I could,' I said, 'but I promised.'

'Promised who?'

'Friend of mine.'

'What friend?' I shook my head.

'Right then,' and he turned away from me. Suddenly the door shut in front of him and Sir Walter Raleigh was standing there, his cane levelled at Will's chest. There was no doubt that Will could see him. You only had to see the look on Will's face. 'Prithee Master Will, no further.' Will backed away towards me.

'Who is it?' His voice was barely audible. 'Who's that man?'

'Cousin Bess, will you not present me to your brother? And make haste to take the bauble from him for I fear he may drop it.' I took the orb from Will's trembling hands.

'This is Sir Walter Raleigh,' I said. 'He's the friend I was telling you about. He's one of our ancestors, remember?' Will was swallowing hard. 'It's all right,' I said. 'He won't hurt. Honest he won't.'

'But he's dead,' said Will pushing me forward and holding me like a shield between himself and my friend Walter. 'He's in the history books,' he whispered. 'He's dead. He's been dead for ages.'

'Three hundred and seventy years this very year,' said Walter, lowering his cane and smiling broadly. 'Be not afeared of me, Master Will. I bear you no ill will. I come to help you, not to harm you.'

'Then he's a ghost?' said Will. 'He's a real live ghost?'

'Real, but unfortunately not live, cousin,' said Walter. 'I am as you say a spirit being, visible only to those I wish to see me. Until now only your sister has seen me and I had promised never to show myself to anyone else.' Walter looked at me and shrugged his shoulders. 'I had no choice, chick. You understand that, do you not? I had to stop your impetuous brother. I could not allow my plan to be discovered. It would have been the end of it. Shall I tell him all, dear cousin?'

I nodded. 'Your sister Bess brought me here from the Tower many long weeks ago, and I lived amongst you all that time though you did not know it. I know you all better than you can imagine, Master Will. You are indeed my family and I have come to love you as such.'

'The letter,' Will whispered, his hands gripping my shoulder so hard it hurt. 'It was him that wrote it then, wasn't it? He's "W.R." He's Walter Raleigh.'

'Aye, that I did, cousin,' Walter sighed, 'and most carelessly left it lying on the table for you to find it. You did not dream it, Master Will. It was I that took away the letter and hid it whilst you were outside the door.'

'And the bottle?' Will asked.

'That was the elixir,' I said.

'The what?' said Will.

'The medicine,' I explained. 'Walter made it down in your chemistry lab – in the cellar. I told you it wasn't me messing about down there, didn't I? It was Walter. He saved her life, Will. He gave me the elixir in the bottle and I gave to Gran in her tea.'

'Then you were the old man she saw in her dreams,' said Will. 'But it wasn't in her dreams at all, was it? And it was you that stole the Crown Jewel. You brought it down with you.'

'Hidden under his cloak,' I said. 'Anything he hides under his cloak you can't see. He hid me twice, didn't you, Walter?' I felt Will's grip on my shoulder loosen somewhat.

'He brought it back with him on the train, but I didn't know anything about it, not then.'

'But why?' said Will. 'What for?'

'For us,' I said. 'Walter did it for us. See, he knows all about the farm, all about us being kicked out and having nowhere to go.'

'I would not have you suffer as I once did,' said Walter. 'I would not allow history to repeat itself. I see I must explain more. They took all that was mine, Master Will, when they called me traitor and condemned me. God, it breaks my brain when I think on it, even now. I was betrayed by my own king; and worse, I was betrayed by those I thought were my friends. I would be avenged for the wrong they did me and the wrong that has been done to you. I was no traitor, Master Will. So you see, I have restored to my family only a small part of what is owed to us. They have baubles and trinkets a-plenty in the Tower – they will not miss it. Faith, it is ours by right Master Will. Why, the very gold and jewels you see before you might have come from a Spanish treasure ship I myself captured. It was mine, I tell you, before it was ever the Crown's, and 'twas most wickedly taken from me. You have but to sell it, and my honour and our family's fortune is restored for ever.'

'I told him already it was too late,' I said, 'that we've got to leave tomorrow.'

'There are other farms,' said Walter, 'and perchance we may yet find a better one –'

'But you *can't* sell it,' said Will, coming out from behind me at last.

'That's what I told him,' I said. 'It's not right. It belongs to the Queen.'

'I don't mean that,' said Will. 'What I mean is no one would buy it, would they? I mean it's like Father said, everyone knows what it looks like, don't they? Everyone'll be on the lookout for it. You can't hardly just walk into a jeweller in Exeter and say "What'll you give me for this?" and then plonk it down on the counter.' And then he thought for a moment. 'But come to think of it, I suppose you could pick out the jewels and melt down the gold.'

'You can't!' I said. 'You wouldn't!' I was horrified at the thought of destroying something so beautiful.

'They'd soon make another one. Just think, Bess, only got to sell it and we could have any farm we wanted.' Then he shook his head. 'But it's no good. We still couldn't sell the gold even if it was just a lump, nor the jewels. I mean just supposing I tried, they'd still wonder where I got it from wouldn't they? Wouldn't work.'

'He's right, Walter,' I said and I held out the orb for Walter. He folded his arms resolutely. 'You've got to take it. You *must*,' I said, a sudden panic rising inside me. 'How are we going to explain it if they find it here? We'll all go to prison, Mother, Father, everyone. You shouldn't have done it, Walter. It's not right to steal things. Just because someone else stole from you first doesn't make it right to steal it back.' Walter looked down at me and his face darkened with anger.

'I had thought better of you, cousin. Do you dare to teach me right from wrong, I who have lived through a lifetime and had hundreds of years to ponder on it, I who have shaped the history of the world? Have you so little faith in me? All I have done I have done for you and you pay me thus with insults. My honour is all I have left and now you would steal even that from me and call me thief. I see you love me not, cousin.'

Will hid behind me again as the onslaught continued. But the anger turned suddenly to hurt. 'In your service, cousin Bess, I have endeavoured much and accomplished little – it is true. But to spurn me so is not generous.'

'I didn't mean it like that,' I said.

'You have no longer any need of your friend Walter,' he went on. 'I see I have disappointed you, and I would not stay where I am not wanted, so I bid you both goodnight and farewell.' And he was gone, vanishing through the door, leaving us both gaping after him, and me still holding the orb.

'Come back Walter, please come back,' I cried. But I knew he would not. I turned to Will. 'Now what are we going to do?' I said.

At that moment I heard a door open along the passage, and there were steps coming along towards my door, Father's footsteps. I leaped into bed quickly, clutching the orb to my stomach. Will switched off the light and hid behind the door – there was nowhere else to hide. The door opened. I squeezed my eyes closed and breathed deeply and regularly. 'Bess, you awake?' said Father. He waited for a moment and then shut the door behind him and went out. 'It's all right, dear,' I heard him say as he went back into their room. 'I told you so. She's fast asleep. Don't you go worrying yourself any more.'

'Thought I heard voices, that's all,' said Mother.

'Well, if you did she's been talking in her sleep again.'

I sat up and Will tiptoed over and sat on my bed. 'Close one,' he said. 'We've got to get that thing out of the house, and quick Bess, before someone finds it. We've got to hide it.'

'What if Walter doesn't come back?' I said.

'Then we'll be stuck with it, won't we? Either way we've got to hide it.'

'In the morning,' I whispered, suddenly feeling very tired.

'Now,' Will insisted. 'There'll be people all over the place in the morning. The removal men are coming at breakfast time, remember? We've got to get it out of the house, and now.'

'If only he hadn't gone off,' I said. 'He could have hidden it under his cloak. I shouldn't have said all those things. He was only doing his best, and when you think about it I suppose he was right – I mean he was only taking back what was his in the first place. And after all, he was only trying to help us, wasn't he?'

'Maybe,' said Will, 'but all he's done is drop us right in the muck.' He paused for a moment. 'I've got it!' he said and he tried to stifle a chuckle. 'I've got it. I've got the perfect place. Come on Bess, quick, and don't drop the orb.'

The floorboards creaked horribly as we crept along the passage and down the stairs but we made it to the front door. (Humph slept in the kitchen too close to the back door so we couldn't go that way.) The bolt was stiff and grated loudly as Will drew it back. The moon was so bright it was like daylight outside. I followed Will who ran on ahead in striped pyjamas, crouching like a commando. My bare feet kept finding all the sharpest stones, so that it was difficult not to cry out with the pain of it. The night was strangely silent, no bleating of sheep, no cows browsing in Front Meadow.

'Here we are,' Will whispered as we reached the orchard.

'Where?' I said.

'There,' he said, pointing at the heap of horse-dung against the hedgerow. 'We'll hide it in there.'

'We can't!' I said.

'Why not? No one would ever think of looking in there would they?' And you couldn't argue with that. 'We'll dig it up in the morning when we've decided what to do with it. Maybe by that time your friend will come back anyway and then he can take it back to London where it belongs.'

He climbed up on to the dungheap with a fencing stake in his hand and plunged it into the heap again and again until he had made a deep hole. 'That'll do,' he said. 'Give it here.' And he took the orb out of my hand and lowered it gently down into the hole.

'Come and give me a hand,' he said. 'We've got to fill it in.'

'I've got nothing on my feet,' I said.

'Nor've I,' said Will. 'It'll wash off.'

And so it did. When we'd finished burying the orb we dunked our feet and hands in the water trough in the cow yard and dabbled them till they were clean again.

'I've been thinking,' said Will. 'I've been thinking about the robbery. It said on the radio that nothing was broken, no glass, nothing. No alarm set off. When you think about it, it's got to be a ghost. I mean he just walked right through your bedroom door, didn't open it or anything, did he? It's what he must have done up there, walked right through the glass and took it. Brilliant. Magic. If I knew how to melt down gold and if we could sell it . . .'

'Will,' I said firmly. 'It's going back.'

'I know,' Will said. 'It's a pity though. You could buy a fair-sized farm with ten million pounds, couldn't you; and have a little left over for a graphite rod. They're the best. I've always wanted a graphite rod.'

'It's cold,' I said, 'and I'm going to bed.'

Back in my room I coughed several times just in case Walter had come back, but he hadn't and he didn't. I wanted to say sorry. I had to find him again to make him understand, to explain what I'd meant.

'Two wrongs don't make a right' – Gran had said it often enough – and now I understood what she meant for the first time. And she was right. But I hadn't meant to upset him like that.

I slept in fits and starts, each time waking up and coughing to see if he was back, but dawn came and I was still alone. As I watched the sun come up over the trees beyond Front Meadow, I knew it was for the last time. Tomorrow morning I'd be waking up at Aunty Ellie's, and all you could see from her windows were houses and lamp-posts and streets. I wasn't really sad though, not any more. I knew we were going and that there was nothing anyone could do to stop it. I suppose I had just become used to the idea. Anyway I had more urgent things on my mind, like what the dickens we were going to do with the golden orb, and about how I was going to get my friend Walter back.

Downstairs I heard Mother talking to Humph and putting him out – you could hear his tail banging against the back door. A little later I heard the sound of the removal van arriving. I didn't much want to be downstairs and watch everything being carried out so I stayed where I was as long as I could. Besides, it was warm in bed and I hated getting up anyway.

Will and I didn't get a chance to talk before breakfast. He

came down after me like he always did. He gave me a long confidential look and winked at me. My brother Will loved a conspiracy. In spite of the packing cases everywhere it was an ordinary enough breakfast, except that Humph wasn't sitting expectantly under Little Jim's highchair. I fed Little Jim his cereal (a kind of puree of porridge), scooping it off his chin and his cheek and shovelling it in again. Mother said Humph was outside begging the removal-men's breakfast.

Father was hitting the top of his boiled egg viciously. 'Vultures, that's what they are, always have been.'

'Who, dear?' Mother said.

'Those Barrowbill twins. It's just like they've been waiting all these years for us to go down the shoot. Did you see what they bought yesterday? Did you? Almost all the pigs, couple of the cows and my favourite tractor, the little Massey 125.'

'Someone had to buy them dear,' said Mother. 'Doesn't much matter who, does it?'

'Sticks in my craw, that's all,' Father went on. 'They've lived across the valley from us for over twenty years and in all that time they've never been anything but trouble. They never keep their fences up – their sheep wander everywhere and the damage their pigs have done over the years doesn't bear thinking about. And did they ever pay a penny piece in compensation? Never. It was like getting blood out of a stone. Still, at least I got their money before they took them away yesterday – cash, too. Paid me a good price for that dung, too,' said Father, picking the shell off the edge of his boiled egg. We looked at him. 'Horse-dung – you know, that heap in the orchard. Well don't look so surprised. You didn't think I'd leave it behind, did you? Valuable stuff, that is – and we could hardly take it with us to Aunty Ellie's now, could we?'

'When are they collecting it?' I asked.

'Done it already. Came first thing this morning and loaded it right up. Said they were going to spread it right now while it's still dry. There's rain on the way, they said – needed it for their vegetable patch.'

'Can we go out?' said Will, wiping his mouth with the back of his hand.

'You haven't finished your breakfast, dear,' said Mother.

'Don't feel like it,' said Will, 'do we?' He looked at me.

'No,' I said, and I meant it. And we were gone out of the door before they could stop us and running hard down towards the orchard. A flurry of rooks flew up as we opened the orchard gate but one or two were still left busy at the worms where the horse-dung heap had once been.

There was no point in even looking, but we did it all the same, searching the ground again and again, just to be sure that the unbelievable terrible worst really had happened. It had. 'Now what?' said Will, kicking a clod of dung into the air.

'Well, at least no one will find it here now,' I said. 'They won't be able to blame us, will they?'

'And what happens when they find it in the dung?' said Will. 'I mean you can't miss it can you, not a thing like that? They'll take it straight to the police, won't they? And they'll tell them where they got the dung from. That's what they'll do, and we'll be dropped right in it. We've got to go after it and get it back before they find it.'

'You have a wise brother, cousin Bess,' said a voice from behind us. My friend Walter was sitting on a tree stump not five yards from us smoking his pipe. 'I' faith 'tis good advice, chick.' He smiled at me. 'You see that I have recovered my good humour. I was always too proud a man for my own good, and perhaps endowed with too excitable a spirit.'

'I only meant . . .'

But he held up his cane and stood up. 'Enough, sweet cousin,' he said. 'I have reflected much through the night and know now that you questioned more my wisdom than mine honour, and my wisdom have I often questioned myself. Come, cousin,' and he held out his hands, 'are we friends again?'

'Course,' I said, and he bent and kissed me on the forehead. 'Master Will,' he said. 'I see you are much like me – intemperate, injudicious,' (Will looked rather puzzled) 'but possessed of a fiery spirit that will not accept defeat. Come, we shall find this bauble if it is there, and when it is found, then indeed it will be left to you both to decide what should be done with it. Are we agreed?' We were.

The quickest way to the Barrowbill's farm was across the river. We forded it together, knee-high in the water holding hands to keep ourselves upright against the current. The stones were slippery underfoot and I should have fallen more than once had my friend Walter not held me up. We clambered up through the woods, Will running on ahead to hurry us along. We stumbled over a ploughed field and at last skirted the hedgerow that ran to the house. I'd been there once or twice in the car with Mother to deliver the parish magazines.

You could smell the dung already. The vegetable garden was to one side of the house and we could not see it. We could only just see the garden fence from where we were. A tractor and trailer were parked near the front gate, and the trailer was quite empty. 'They've spread it already,' said Will, stating the obvious. We waited for a few moments debating if it was safe to search the front garden. The 'horrible Barrowbills' did not like trespassers and did not like children – we knew that well enough from past experience. 'What are we going to say to them if they catch us?' said Will. 'We can't hardly tell them what we're looking for, can we?'

'Master Will,' said Walter. 'Perchance you have forgotten that I may go unseen where I will. They shall not see me unless I wish it. I pray you rest here awhile and watch. If I find the bauble I shall bring it back to you, you can be sure of it.' And he walked out across the yard, limping and leaning heavily on his cane.

'Why does he limp?' Will asked.

'He told me he was wounded in the leg when he was capturing Cadiz from the Spanish,' I said. 'And he was, too – I read it in a book I've got. He got a wooden splinter in it when a cannon ball hit his ship.'

We saw him open the gate and then walk up and down the vegetable garden prodding at the dung with his cane. Once in a while he would stop and bend down so that he all but disappeared from our view, but when he stood up again he would shake his head in our direction.

'But it's got to be there,' Will said, biting on his wrist. 'It's got to be.'

'P'raps they've found it already,' I said. It was almost as though Walter heard me because he suddenly stopped in his tracks and looked towards the house as if he'd heard something. Only one small window looked out on the vegetable garden. Walter walked over to it and peered in. He rubbed the window and looked again, his face against the glass. Then he was waving his cane to us and beckoning us over.

We left the cover of the hedge and ran low across the yard and into the vegetable garden, a trio of hens scurrying away as we came. I followed slipping and slithering on the horse-dung that clung to the bottom of my wellingtons. Walter was pointing at the window, his finger to his lips. We rose from below the window slowly until our eyes were over the windowsill and we could see everything. The 'horrible Barrowbills' had their backs to us. They were standing by the kitchen sink and the tap was running. They were washing something, and it wasn't their hands. We could only catch a glimpse of it, but it was golden and it was round, and they were washing it carefully, very carefully indeed.

# CHAPTER 9

'WELL, THAT'S IT,' I WHISPERED AND WE DUCKED down below the window. 'We'll never get it back now.'

'What if I went and knocked at the front door?' said Will, 'then you could sneak in the back way and grab it.'

'There's two of them,' I said. 'They won't both answer the door, will they?'

Will thought for a moment. 'You could always chuck a stone through a window round the front,' he said. 'They'd soon come running then, both of them.'

'You can't!' I said, though I must admit I quite liked the idea of it.

'Faith, dear Bess,' said Walter smiling broadly, 'you have too kind a heart, too generous a spirit. Have you not often told me of these men? Did they not shout at you and drive you off their land? Did they not shoot at your dog? What's one broken window after all that? A broken window is but a trifle and can be afterwards mended.'

'A trifle?' said Will. 'What does he mean, a trifle?' I didn't know what Walter meant either, but I could guess. After all I was more used to his strange language than Will was.

Walter crouched down beside us. 'You have something of the pirate in you, Master Will,' he said. 'Would that I had you by my side at Cadiz when we burnt the Spanish fleet, or when the Armada came and we harried them up the Channel. I had need of such men as you in those days.' He peered in through the window once more. 'But I think I may have a way to resolve this, cousin Bess; and moreover we might do it in such a way that we would have no need to break any windows.' He was smiling wickedly. 'Watch at the window, I pray, and you shall see that I can whine and scream and jabber as well as any other ghost if I choose to.'

A few minutes later he was no longer beside us but standing in the kitchen behind the 'horrible Barrowbills' who were still bent over the sink together. Walter turned and winked at us. He was smiling like a naughty boy. I saw him take a deep breath and very slowly and deliberately he lifted his arms up inside his cloak so that he looked like a giant black bat, a vampire bat, and then he let out the most hideous skin-crawling cry I have ever heard. It echoed around the house before dying away to a whining, tremulous whimper. Behind us the chickens flew up out of the vegetable garden in a panic. The 'horrible Barrowbills' had turned and were backing away along the kitchen wall. I felt sorry for them – honestly I did. Worse was to come, though, for as Walter advanced slowly towards them arms outstretched, his hands reached up towards his head, and took it off.

'Cripes!' said Will beside me.

But my friend Walter hadn't finished with them yet. He tucked his head under his arm, glared at them through baleful red-rimmed eyes and set up a soft cooing sound that wound itself up into a reverberating ululation that shook the crockery on the dresser. All this time I had not looked at the horrible Barrowbills but I did now. Bertie was clinging to Boney's arm (or perhaps it was the other way round – I could never tell them apart), his face screwed up with terror, and Boney was trying to push him off as he edged away from Sir Walter towards the door.

The golden orb must still be in the sink, I thought, for neither of them had it with them. In their scramble to get to the door Bertie knocked against the dresser and brought cups and plates crashing down to the ground around him. Boney tripped over a chair and almost fell out of the room after the other one. Cursing and roaring, they tore out of the house and we heard them running up the footpath towards the gate. A car engine started. Gears crashed, wheels spun and they were gone up the lane, a cloud of dust rising behind them. You could hardly blame them. I mean *I* was terrified, and I knew it was only my friend Walter playing games, my friend Walter who wouldn't harm a fly; and as for Will – and remember he knew Walter quite well by now, too – Will had fainted clean away beside me and was lying in a crumpled heap at my feet.

By the time I'd shaken him to his senses Walter had his head on again. 'I fear I may have been overly enthusiastic,' he said, walking through the wall and kneeling down beside us. He took out a bottle from his waistcoat. 'I keep it by me always,' he said. 'It is my own remedy. Do you not recall, good cousin, 'twas this that revived you when first we met in the Bloody Tower those many weeks past?' How could I ever forget! 'It worked well enough for you then,' he went on, 'and now it will restore your brother. Have faith.'

And indeed it did. Within a few moments Will was sitting back against the wall and his eyes blinked open. He coughed until his eyes ran with tears and he pushed away the bottle from his face. He looked at both of us. 'Have they gone?' he asked. I nodded.

'You fainted,' I said, and with some satisfaction.

'Well you can't hardly blame me, can you,' said Will. 'You might have told me you were going to take your head off like that, Walter.'

'My humblest apologies, Master Will,' said Walter. 'They

will not be back for some time though, I think. I wanted to be quite sure they would not have the time nor the inclination to take the bauble with them.'

'You've got it then?' said Will pushing himself up on to his elbows.

'I have it,' said Sir Walter, but there was a certain tone in his voice and he did not look very pleased or relieved about it. He sighed. 'I fear however it is not quite as we expected,' he said, and he opened his cloak and held out a shining brass ball with a short length of pipe attached to it.

'What the dickens is that?' I asked taking it from him. 'It's not the orb.'

'It's one of those, you know those thingummyjigs,' said Will, searching for the word he wanted. 'You know a thingummyjig . . . a ball something . . . a ballcock. You see them in all the drinking troughs out in the fields. It's got to be somewhere. It can't just disappear, can it?' We all stood up and began to search again through the vegetable patch. 'Still,' said Will turning over the dung with his feet, 'it was good to see Bertie and Boney scared rigid. Father would have loved that. At least I didn't faint till after I'd seen that. You were brilliant, Walter. Wicked, wasn't he, Bess?'

'Wicked?' said Walter somewhat perplexed and almost offended.

'Cool,' said Will. 'Y'know bril, magic, wicked.' Walter looked none the wiser.

'We still haven't found the orb, have we?' I said. 'And if we don't find it someone else will.'

Walter had picked up something from the ground. It looked at first like a mucky carrot or a rotten turnip. ' 'Tis a bone, cousin, and I have noticed that there are many others here.' He prodded his cane to the ground and flicked a blackened ball towards us. 'In truth I think the heap was a burial ground for that dog of yours that follows me like a shadow everywhere I go.'

'Humph!' I said. 'Of course! That's it! He's always digging in there and coming back to the house stinking to high heaven. Perhaps he's found the orb and dug it up and buried it somewhere.'

It was a fairly forlorn hope, I admit, but it was the only one we had left. We had a last look around the Barrowbills' vegetable garden just in case we had missed it. We found a lot more bones and a dead rat, but no golden orb. So empty-handed and not a little dejected we made our way back down through the woods across the river and up to the farm again. The removal men were still hard at it, huffing and puffing back and forth with Father scurrying about organising everyone. Mother was so busy between making cups of tea, feeding Little Jim and wrapping everything in newspaper for the tea-chests that she didn't even notice us as we came in.

'Looking for Humph,' said Will. 'You seen him, Mother?' And he pocketed a handful of biscuits from the table.

'I shut him in the shed,' she said. 'He bit one of the removal men on the ankle. I think he knows we're going – he's not himself at all.' I gave Little Jim a kiss on his cheek which was clean for a change and he nearly tore my ear off. What is it that he likes so much about ears and noses? I managed to escape his clutches by offering him one of the biscuits Will had left behind on the table, and then I ran out after Will. I expected Mother or Father to ask us to do something to help, but perhaps they were glad to have us out from under their heels that day. Anyway it was always a good idea to be out of the way when Father was frantic, and he was frantic now, I can tell you.

In the end we found Humph curled up at the back of Sally's stable on a paper sack. He was looking very sorry for himself and he was clearly delighted to see us all. He started squeaking like a wild thing when he saw who it was, jumping up and down at Walter like a bouncing ball, and driving him up against the wall of the stable. Will retrieved him and tried to talk to him which was useless because Humph didn't even know what 'Sit' meant. Anyway he wasn't used to being sensible with Will – he was used to playing the idiot and so he couldn't change no matter how hard Will tried to calm him down. 'You know where it is Humph, don't you?' Will said. 'Course you do. There's a good dog. You just show us where you buried it and you can have all these biscuits.' And Will held a handful of biscuits above his nose. You could see that

Humph wasn't the least bit interested in the deal. Of course he wanted the biscuits all right, but you'd expect that with any dog.

'Miserable cur,' said Walter brushing down his paw-marked cloak.

'It's no good,' I said.

'Nothing ventured nothing gained,' said Will – another of Gran's favourites.

'You've just got to let him out and then we'll follow him,' I said.

Will seemed to think that was a good idea. 'Seek!' he said, opening the door and pointing Humph's muzzle in the direction of the orchard. 'Seek!'

Well, of course Humph went out of the stable like a bullet and the last we saw of him he was crawling under the gate out into Sally's field. We tried to follow him but he was gone. Whistling was no good, but Will tried it anyway. He tried using his commanding voice, then his wheedling voice, then his angry voice, but Humph never came back no matter what voice he used.

We asked one of the removal men (the one in the woolly bobble hat) if they'd seen him and he said that if he saw him again he'd kick him from here to kingdom come. We guessed he might be the one Humph had bitten on the ankle. He was not very helpful at all, but then I suppose you could hardly blame him. The other one who had his shirt off was tattooed with anchors and naked ladies from the wrist to the shoulders on both arms. He was a bit more friendly and he said he thought he'd seen Humph out in the orchard. We went to check but he wasn't there. Walter decided he would go off looking for Humph on his own – we'd cover more ground that way, he said. It made sense.

By lunchtime we still had not found Humph, and Will and I sat outside on the garden wall and ate our sandwiches and crisps and just waited for Humph to come back. We knew Humph could be anywhere; he was probably off rabbiting somewhere. Sometimes he'd go off for the whole day if there were a lot of rabbits about. Or perhaps Walter had found him and would bring him back.

In the removal van we could see them reading their papers and pouring tea out of a thermos. They had their radio on loudly. When they got out of the cab after lunch they were arguing. 'And I'm telling you it was an inside job,' said the one in the hat. 'I've been up to the Tower of London. It's like flaming Fort Knox in there. You'd have to blast your way in there with gelignite or dynamite and they didn't, did they?'

'You've got to know your electronics, that's all,' said the one with tattoos, scratching himself on his wobbly stomach. 'All you got to do is cut off the system and then you can get in and take out what you like.'

'That's my point, though. You've got to know the system before you can nobble it,' said the other one. 'Stands to reason, doesn't it? I mean all this talk about the "impregnable fortress" is a lot of old hogwash. Nothing's that impossible. You just think about it. All you need is one crooked Beefeater, who knows his way around, and you're in. And I'll tell you another thing, they won't never find it again neither – melted down by now and out of the country.'

The scratching one thought for a moment. 'P'raps the Queen took it herself,' he said. 'You know, perhaps she borrowed it for the day without telling anyone. I mean it's hers after all, isn't it? She doesn't have to tell anyone does she?'

'You daft hiccup,' said the one in the woolly bobble hat, 'I'll tell you what though, have you seen that colour picture on the front page? It's a bit special isn't it? Wouldn't mind that on my mantelpiece, I can tell you.'

'You haven't got a mantelpiece.'

'I'd build one specially for it.'

'Come on, let's get this lot finished. It's getting late.' And they were almost inside the house by now when the scratching one turned round and called out to us: 'I seen that dog of yours. Looks as if he's digging something up in the flower garden.'

Will and me, we never finished our sandwiches. We found Humph in the flower garden just like the removal man said, and he *was* digging something up; but it wasn't the orb. I shan't tell you what it was because it was too revolting. But anyway we'd found him, and so we stalked him after that keeping our distance and watching him as he dug in the hedgerows for rabbits, as he prowled the hay barns for rats. He chased the black cat out of the woodshed and up a tree. He ferreted in the dustbin until he came out with some cheese rind which he chewed, eyes closed with ecstasy on the front lawn.

Time was running out. The removal van was loaded and ready to go. We would be off in half an hour, Mother said. In a last ditch attempt Will lured Humph to the orchard leaving a trail of crisps and sandwich crusts and biscuits, and he snuffled round where the old dung-heap had been but it was obviously of no real interest to him. In the end he went off to his mattress of dry leaves under the diesel tank, tucked himself up and went to sleep. I could have killed him, I really could.

Walter suddenly appeared beside us as we sat silently on the garden wall waiting until the time came to leave. It was strange, really. He didn't seem at all gloomy about the failure of our search. On the contrary he shrugged it all off rather jauntily, I thought. We would find it again, he said. He was sure of it.

Mr Watts drove up to see us before we left, to wish us good luck, he said. He leaned in through the Landrover door to offer us a last humbug. Will snatched the whole packet out of his hand. 'Humph likes them,' he said. (That was true.

Humph liked them just as much as he did.) It was a frosty goodbye after that and Mother said we would have to have better manners at Aunty Ellie's, but Will never answered. He was looking out of the back window at the farm as the Landrover drove away, and I could see there were silent tears streaming down his face. Beside him Humph waited for the next humbug, and beside me sat my friend Walter puffing thoughtfully on his pipe. I couldn't cry a single tear. I felt as if I should but I couldn't. The farm didn't matter to me any more, nor the house. What's done is done, as Gran would say. The golden orb from the Crown Jewels was all that mattered now. We had to find it. We just had to. And then it occurred to me that maybe they'd find it some day in the future where Humph had buried it out on the farm and Mr Watts would be accused and condemned and sent to the Tower for ever. That would be justice, I thought. That would serve him right. And that cheered me up no end as we drove down the lane and away.

Aunty Ellie greeted us with one of her famous teas. There were plates of scones and sandwiches and chocolate cakes and of course cream, lashings of cream with everything; and Gran, who seemed quite recovered now, bustled about us trying to comfort Mother and Father who both looked pale and exhausted. I coughed four times. My friend Walter was wandering around the room looking at the pictures and admiring himself in the mirror. He liked doing that a lot, I noticed. Then, irritatingly, he disappeared through a wall and I didn't see him again.

Gran prattled on merrily. 'Of course when Ellie told me you might have to leave the farm I was a little upset, but not as much as you might think. To be honest with you, I felt the place was a millstone around your necks. Scrimping and saving all those years to keep it going. Running hard only to stand still, that's what it was. Lovely for the children of course, but there's other places, Will,' she said, kissing Will on top of his head. 'Every cloud has a silver lining dear, you'll see.' And at that we all smiled together and laughed, and Gran was so delighted she had managed to lift our sunken spirits. 'I never said so at the time,' she went on much encouraged, 'but I never liked the farm very much, except Sally of course. There were always flies in the summer – millions of them, and all of them in my room. And in the winter there was the smell of that silage and well . . . you know what . . . indescribable, indescribable.' And she went on to describe it at length. Aunty Ellie stopped her in the end because Humph was scratching to be let out of the door. 'He'll have to go on a lead,' Aunty Ellie said firmly.

'But he's never been on a lead, Aunty,' I said. 'He's a country dog.'

'Well, he'll have to go on one here, country dog or not. He's a town dog for the moment and he's going to have to learn town ways. You don't want him run over, do you?'

Father said he'd like to walk off his tea so we all three gathered in the front hall with Humph, and Aunty Ellie gave Father the lead. 'I'll take him,' said Father clipping it on Humph's collar. As it turned out it was the other way round. Humph took him.

It was a tug of war from the start and Humph never let up, not for one moment. He dragged Father down the road so fast that he had to trot and we had to run flat out just to keep up. 'Go round the block,' Aunty Ellie had told us. 'Turn right and right and right again and that will bring you back home. It takes about ten minutes.' And so we did. As we ran it occurred to me that my friend Walter might not be with us, and even if he was that he wouldn't be able to keep up this pace. I slowed to a stop and coughed for him. I coughed again and looked back up the road. He wasn't with us. I shouted for Will to stop and beckoned him back to me. 'It's Walter,' I said, breathing hard. 'Must've left him behind.'

'You called him?' he asked. I nodded. 'He'll come,' said Will. 'He always comes in the end. You should know that by now. Come on.' And we ran on again as Humph and Father disappeared around the corner ahead of us.

Then we heard Father shouting. 'What are you up to? Come here! Come here!' At first we thought he was shouting for us to hurry up, so we began to run faster. His bellowing filled the streets. Curtains moved and faces appeared at windows. Doors opened and heads popped up over hedges.

We rounded the corner to find Father getting to his feet, a broken lead in his hand. 'It just snapped,' he said, brushing himself down angrily. 'That infernal dog. I'll get him. I'll get him. Come back here you beggar!' And he charged after Humph, who had stopped two lamp-posts away and was doing his best to push his head through a hedge, pawing at the ground and whining hysterically. Father got there first. He grabbed Humph by the collar and hauled him back. He was just tying up the two ends of the lead when he dropped to his knees by the hedge. By the time we got there he was reaching through the hedge and brushing away at the leaves underneath it. When he stood up he was holding a small hessian sack in his hand.

Two or three people had come out of their garden gates to see what all the commotion was about and were standing on the pavement on the opposite side of the road. Father told us to hold the dog for him, so I hung on to Humph by the collar, which was not easy. He opened the sack and peered inside. 'Cripes,' he said and he reached in and pulled out the golden orb from the Crown Jewels. I felt Will nudge me. Over the top of the hedge we could see into the park beyond, and there stood my friend Walter, legs crossed and leaning against a tree. He was looking almightily pleased with himself.

# CHAPTER 10

I DON'T KNOW WHERE ALL THE PEOPLE CAME from, but every new street seemed to swell the crowd so that by the time we approached the police station in the centre of town there must have been a hundred people or more in the cavalcade.

Humph led the way, his lead dragging along behind him on the ground, and he was accompanied now by a gang of ragged town dogs all eager to share in the celebrations. Behind them came Father, holding the golden orb in front of him in both hands. Will and I walked on either side of him catching each other's eye from time to time, and each time confirming to each other that there was nothing we could do any more, that events had taken their own course. Of course we both understood – well, I did anyway – that our friend

Walter had somehow set the whole thing up. Why else would he have been standing there behind that hedge and grinning like a Cheshire cat? It wasn't difficult to work out. After all, he knew we were coming that way. He must have been there when Aunty Ellie had told us to go round the block, and he'd just lain in wait for us. It was no accident that the orb had been found lying under the hedgerow – because he'd put it there. And if that was so and it was, then that meant he'd had it all the time we'd been looking for it, or at any rate he'd known all along where it was. And that meant he intended Humph to find it there, but why? What was he up to? I thought he wanted us to sell it and get the money to buy a new farm. That was his plan wasn't it? That's what he'd told us anyway.

I kept looking round to see if Walter was behind us, but if he was I could not find him in the throng of people. The last I had seen of him he was walking away through the trees on the other side of that fence shaking his head and laughing. I ground my teeth. What was he up to? I'd have a thing or two to say to my friend Walter when I caught up with him. Still, at least the orb had been found and at least no one would think we had stolen it. I mean, we'd hardly be handing it in to the police if we'd stolen it, would we?

Then I thought of that whole charade up at the horrible Barrowbills' farmhouse, and how he'd frightened them half to death. It had been a game, to him, just a game. He must have known all the time it couldn't have been the orb in that sink. He must have done because he already knew where it was, wherever that was. It made my blood boil to think how he'd fooled us all.

I was still seething when we at last reached the police station. Someone had obviously warned them we were coming, for there were half a dozen policemen running out to meet us as we climbed up the steps. The crowds were held back and kept in the street whilst we were escorted into the police station. Humph tried to follow us but was grabbed by the collar and turned away at the door. Father put that right at once. 'You'd better let him in,' he said. 'He doesn't look much, but if it weren't for him I wouldn't have found it.' And so Humph padded into the police station alongside me and we were ushered straight into an office.

The policeman who was sitting at the other side of the desk looked at the orb and then at us and then back at the orb again. He couldn't quite take it in. We recognised each other at once. 'Gracious me, it's Mr Throckmorton again, isn't it?' he said. 'Inspector Davidson, you remember? We met yesterday didn't we?' Father nodded, and the Inspector went on, 'We seem to be meeting a lot lately. First there was the stolen horse that mysteriously came back on its own, and then there was your little girl that came back on her own. And now this. You keep us quite busy, sir, don't you? I think you'd better put that thing down whilst I call Headquarters. I have a feeling they'd like to hear about this. Sit down, sit down.' And so we did, including Humph. 'Now tell me, where did you find it?' And Father told him the whole story, which took some time because he left nothing out. The Inspector shook his head throughout. 'Incredible,' he said when Father had finished. 'Quite incredible. And you said there were witnesses?'

'Witnesses?' said Father.

'When your dog found it, Mr Throckmorton, there were other people in the road, you said. They would have seen you then, wouldn't they? They would have seen you finding it.'

'Of course,' said Father. 'There were several of them.' I could see he was getting quite upset. 'Look here, Constable . . .'

'Inspector.'

'Beg your pardon. Look here, Inspector,' Father went on, 'if I say we found it in the hedge at the bottom of the road, then we found it in the hedge at the bottom of the road. I wouldn't hardly have brought it here if I hadn't found it, would I? I mean I couldn't have, could I?'

'Hardly,' said the Inspector smiling. 'But witnesses can help in these matters, you know. Puts the records straight, so to speak. And particularly if there's . . .' He paused for some moments. 'But perhaps you haven't heard, then.'

'Heard what?' Father was bewildered – we all were.

'Well, I never. You haven't heard, have you?' And he

chuckled to himself. 'I'll tell you in just a minute, sir.' He picked up the telephone. 'But first I must phone the Chief Constable. Get me the Chief Constable and double quick,' he said, smiling at us. He put his hand over the mouthpiece. 'You're sure it's the real thing, Mr Throckmorton?' he said, still chuckling.

'I'm not an expert,' said Father, 'but it looks like it to me.'

'Don't suppose there's more than one of them about,' said the Inspector. 'Chief Constable,' he spoke slightly differently now, more pompously. 'Chief Constable. It's Davidson here, sir. Davidson, from Honiton. You're not going to believe this sir, but we've found it . . . the golden orb sir, the Crown Jewel . . . yes, sir, it's sitting on the desk right in front of me . . . Yes, sir, I am quite sure.' He leaned forward and examined the orb. 'No damage so far as I can see, sir . . . No, no jewels missing, don't think so anyway. Looks good as new to me sir . . . Who found it? It's a Mr Throckmorton sir . . . yes sir, it is an unusual name isn't it? Out walking his dog he was . . . Lucky? I'll say so sir. Trouble is I've got half the town outside the station, sir. Newspapers are probably on to it already, and television. I'll need an armoured van and an escort to get it back to London, and more men. I'll need more men on the ground.' He looked at his wrist watch. 'Very well sir, I'll look after it until then. Yes, sir . . . Thank you, sir . . . Goodbye to you, sir.' And he put the phone down, clasped his hands on his desk and looked directly at us. 'Well, Mr Throckmorton, I think you are about to become a very famous person. You are all going to be more famous than you ever dreamed. If I'm not much mistaken, by tonight this town will be full of the world's press and television.'

Father was on his feet. 'If it's all the same to you Inspector, I think we'd better be getting home now. They'll be wondering what's happened to us. I mean, we were just taking the dog out for a ten-minute walk. Come on, you two, and bring Humph with you.' Father bent over the golden orb and examined it fondly, almost as if he was saying goodbye to it. 'Pretty isn't it?' he said. 'Weighs a bit too, I can tell you. So that's what ten million pounds looks like. Ah well, easy come, easy go, as Gran says.' And he laughed and patted it affectionately.

We were almost out of the door when the Inspector called us back. 'Just a moment, Mr Throckmorton,' he said. 'Can we find you at the farm if we want you?'

' 'Fraid not,' said Father. 'We moved out today. We're staying in town for a bit.'

'What address?' Inspector Davidson asked.

Father thought for a bit and then looked at me for help.

'Number twelve Huntley Gardens,' I said.

'Thing is, sir, we'll need to know where to find you.'

'Why's that?'

'Well it's like this, sir – I was about to tell you before I phoned Headquarters. I was about to tell you about the reward.'

'Reward?' said Father.

'Yes, Mr Throckmorton. They announced it this afternoon. There's a reward for any information leading to the recovery of the orb. I'd say it's highly likely you'd qualify for that reward, Mr Throckmorton. You or your dog anyway, and it'll be a tidy sum, Mr Throckmorton.'

'How tidy?' Father asked, swallowing hard.

'A quarter of a million.'

'A quarter of a million pounds?' asked Father.

'That's right sir. Two hundred and fifty thousand pounds,' said the Inspector. Father reached for a nearby chair and clutched it to steady himself. 'Could I have a cup of tea?' he said. 'I feel a bit weak.'

Will and I looked across at each other and we both understood. I coughed twice, and then four times, but if Walter was in the room he wasn't showing himself.

'Walter Raleigh!' Will shouted suddenly, and he threw his arms round Father's neck and hugged him. Of course Humph began barking at that and chased his lead around and around until he pounced on it.

'Pardon?' said the Inspector.

'Oh . . .' Will recovered quickly. 'It's a sort of a new swear word, instead of the ones you aren't allowed to say. You know, when you're excited. You know. Walter Raleigh!' He'd got a nerve, my brother.

'Oh, I see,' said the Inspector. 'Walter Raleigh! Rather good, that. Walter Raleigh! Haven't heard that one before. Walter Raleigh! Rolls well off the tongue too . . . Walter Raleigh!'

'Father,' said Will pulling on his arm, 'we can get ourselves our own farm now, can't we? It's what you always wanted.'

'Don't you go counting your chickens,' said Father and he looked up at the Inspector. 'So that's why you asked whether there were any witnesses, Inspector? I mean, if I'd stolen it myself I'd know where to find it again, wouldn't I, and then I could claim the reward couldn't I? I didn't steal it, Inspector.' Father held up his hand. 'Not guilty, Inspector, Scout's honour.'

'I didn't think you did sir, not really. After all I was out at your place yesterday, the day of the robbery, looking for your daughter, wasn't I? I was there when your runaway daughter phoned and I was there with you when you met her at the station. 'Course –' and he looked right at me – 'Course, she could've done it and brought it back with her from London.' And the two of them heaved with laughter at the thought of it. I managed a thin smile which was the best I could do under the circumstances. Will never even managed that much.

We had a police car to drive us back to Aunty Ellie's and it was just as well because they had to clear a path through the crowd outside to get us through. The hero of the hour – Humph – sat between Will and me in the back seat chewing his lead, oblivious to the cheering and clapping outside. I loved it, and so did Will. He couldn't stop giggling all the way back to Aunty Ellie's.

Father broke the news beautifully, in such a matter-of-fact voice. He went into the hallway of the house and called them. He said he was sorry he'd been gone longer than expected but that Humph had just found the golden orb from the Crown Jewels in a hedgerow; and that was not all, he said, there could be a small reward too, just a quarter of a million pounds. There was a moment of hollow silence and then they all cried like babies. Some people are very strange.

'See, I told you,' said Gran wiping the tears off her cheeks. 'I told you there's a light at the end of every tunnel.'

'Yes Gran,' said Mother, 'and age before beauty, and waste not want not, and a stitch in time saves nine, and where there's a will there's a way.' And they all pointed at Will and laughed till they cried again.

Within half an hour we were besieged in the house by reporters and television cameras. They photographed us for hours outside the front door under the bright lights they'd set up and we all had to cuddle Humph. (He couldn't understand it – all this sudden affection.) Mother and Aunty Ellie had groomed him till he glistened so that he looked really quite presentable for his press conference. They tried to make him bark into the microphone, but he wouldn't; and they asked us the same questions again and again and again. How old were we? Where did we got to school? What was it like to find the Crown Jewels? What was it like to be famous? And then the most common question of all: 'What will you do with all the reward money Mr Throckmorton?'

'Perhaps we'll buy ourselves a farm,' said Father. 'We'd like a place of our own, wouldn't we?'

And that made the headlines in most of the papers the next day. 'Gold sniffing sheepdog finds Crown Jewel in hedgerow. "We'll be able to buy a farm of our own now," says Farmer Throckmorton.'

It was ten days before it all died down and we were left on our own again. They were ten days of endless visits to television and radio studios in London and Plymouth, where everyone smiled at us and gave us sweets, and Humph got brushed at least three times a day. Gran and Aunty Ellie had their hair done every single day. Mother hated it all, and said it was like being in a zoo, and if she had to answer any more questions she would scream.

At school too we were celebrities. In Assembly one morning the headmaster called us both up to the platform and asked Will to tell everyone about it. (I don't know why he didn't ask me.) Will exaggerated – well he would, wouldn't he? – especially the bit about how he'd seen the sack first and helped Humph to drag it out of the hedgerow. Anyway they all cheered when he'd finished and I was surprised at how many new friends I suddenly had. Of course, my teacher launched us all into drawing pictures of the orb and Humph, and she picked out mine as being the best and the most brilliant (which it was) and pinned it up in the front hall of the school where only the best pictures go. Well, it should have been the best, shouldn't it? After all, I had been closer to it than anyone else at school except Will, and he couldn't paint to save his life.

In all that time we never saw my friend Walter. Time and again we coughed for him, Will and I. We went out into the garden, we went into every room in the house. We went 'around the block' with Humph five or six times a day, and we coughed for him and we called him. He was nowhere; or if he was somewhere he wasn't letting us know. We knew how much we owed him. He'd been right all along. Everything had turned out just as he'd said it would, and he hadn't even given us the chance to say thank you. Besides there were a few things I still didn't quite understand. Surely he wouldn't just go off like that without saying goodbye. But as the days passed it certainly looked like it.

Then something happened that gave us reason to believe that my friend Walter was still very much with us, and that he was still weaving his web – if you know what I mean. I never saw him myself, and neither did Will; but Mother did – though of course she didn't know it. He's a cunning old spider, my friend Walter.

# CHAPTER 11

EVER SINCE FATHER TOLD THE WORLD HE wanted to buy a farm the post box at Aunty Ellie's had been full of letters from estate agents and farmers offering this farm or that for sale. Father didn't like the look of any of them. He wanted a farm not too far away, a couple of hundred acres or more, and good buildings. He hadn't liked anything he'd seen so far and he was becoming quite dispirited. Anyway, as Gran kept reminding us we mustn't go putting the cart before the horse or start counting our chicks before they were hatched. After all, we hadn't yet had the reward money.

Then one Saturday morning Mother came back from the shops pushing Little Jim and running up the front path; going like a train she was. Now that was very unusual, because Mother would never run if she could possibly avoid it, and anyway she'd often told us never to run while we were pushing Little Jim in his pram. It was too dangerous, she'd said. She was all excited and couldn't get her coat off before she told us. 'I think I may have found the perfect place, dear,' she said to Father who was still opening the pile of post in the kitchen. She sat down at the table and pushed the letters aside and went on, 'You've got to listen. He said it's only just come on to the market. Thatched house, couple of hundred good acres just like you wanted.'

'Wait a minute, wait a minute,' said Father. 'How d'you find out about it? Who told you?'

'This man, this old man I met. He was sitting on the bench outside the church feeding the birds, and he said he recognised me from my picture in the newspapers. Strange-looking old man he was, kind of old-fashioned in a long black coat and a stick, but most polite. Anyway, he said he knew of a farm a few miles away which was up for sale. Good land, he said.'

'Walter Raleigh!' said Will. Mother looked at him somewhat bewildered. Father assured her that it was just a new-fangled expletive. 'Instead of "Cripes",' he said.

Mother seemed satisfied with that and went on, 'Well, this old man, he told me he was born and brought up there. Best farm in the world, he said. Said we should go and look at it right away, soon as we could, before someone else snaps it up. He was such a sweet old man, dear. He said how we were such a fine-looking family, and he talked all about you two children.' She turned to Will and me. 'Y'know it was almost as if he knew you, the way he spoke about you. Uncanny it was. He said he'd like to think of you growing up on the same farm he'd grown up on. And then your children could stay there and then their children and then their children. He'd like that, he said. And then he just upped and went off. He had a terrible limp, poor old man.'

'Did you get a name?' asked Father.

'He never said his name,' said Mother. 'I never asked.'

'Not him. The farm, dear. What's the farm called?'

'Ooh, I've got that somewhere, I wrote it down. He made me write it down.' And she fished in her shopping basket and pulled out an envelope. 'I put it on the bottom of my shopping list. Where is it? Where is it? Ah, here it is. It's called, let me see, I can't read my own writing these days. It's called Hayes Barton, near East Budleigh. Not far from the sea, he said.'

I knew it. I knew it. I didn't have to search the back of my brain. The moment Mother said the old man had been born there I knew the rest. So that was his plan. That had been his plan all along, to buy back his own birthplace, to keep it in the family.

I thought it all out in the car on the way to Hayes Barton that afternoon. I thought back to the great family gathering Aunty Ellie had taken me to in that hotel by the Tower, how no one knew who had invited everyone. It was him, my friend Walter. It must have been. And hadn't he said again and again how he would have his revenge, how he would take back what was rightly his? Hadn't he promised me he would put his family back where they belong? But why me I wondered? There were lots of other relations at that party. Why had he chosen me?

I knew before we ever saw Hayes Barton that Father and Mother would love the place on sight. And they did. I knew there would be room enough for Will and me, for Little Jim and Gran, and for Aunty Ellie when she came to stay; and there was. The fields and hills around were lush and green, even after a dry October. It was a fine farm, the best farm in the world, just like he'd told Mother.

The owners weren't there (they'd already left, it seemed); but we were shown round by a neighbouring farmer who said the house needed a lot doing to it. It looked wonderful to me, though I did see a lot of spiders in the bedrooms and one whopper in the bath that scurried down the plughole when Humph jumped up to look; but spiders apart it was as Mother had said, perfect. We walked the farm from end to end and Father seemed to like what he saw better and better with every stop.

We were getting back into the car when the farmer led Father away by the elbow to speak to him confidentially. He didn't take him far enough because I could hear every word he said, and so could Will – but then, of course we *were* listening rather hard. 'Course I don't want to put you off Mr Throckmorton, but there's been talk, you know.'

'Talk?'

'Well,' said the farmer whose flat tweed hat was so thick with age and sweat and dirt that it sat stiff as a board on his head. 'I don't like to say this, doesn't seem fair to them that's just left, but I got to be fair to you. You're a farmer like myself. After all I've got no axe to grind, have I?' His voice dropped even lower and he looked over his shoulder before he spoke again. 'Well, you may not believe this, but it was the ghost that drove them off. They told me as much themselves.'

'The ghost?'

'It's true, honest it is. It drove their tractors off. It left gates open. It started up the milking parlour in the middle of the night.' Father laughed. 'You can laugh, but they saw it.'

'Saw it?' said Father.

The farmer nodded. 'Headless, they said. It walked headless up and down the passage every night, moaning and groaning like goodness knows what. They couldn't sleep, not a wink. Every night, it was. And it was him they said.'

'Him?'

'That Walter Raleigh. He was born here you see. Lived here, he did. And in the end they chopped off his head. They said he'd come back to haunt the place.'

Father roared with laughter and clapped the farmer on the shoulder. 'I've heard some stories in my time,' he said, 'but that takes the biscuit.'

The farmer looked a bit put out. 'All right, but don't say I didn't warn you, that's all.' Father turned away still laughing and got into the car.

'What was all that about?' Mother asked.

'He was rabbiting on about some ghost haunting the place – lot of old nonsense. Don't believe in ghosts myself. Never have done. He probably wants the place for himself – good block of land next to his own, with a good house on it. He wants it for himself, the cunning old codger.'

'Still,' said Mother, 'we'd better not say anything to Gran about it, had we? We don't want her having one of her turns again, do we. Which room do you think she ought to have?'

'Oh we're taking it are we, then?' said Father smiling. 'We're moving in, are we?'

'Yes, we are, dear,' said Mother. 'You know we are. We all know we are, don't we, children?'

Father nodded slowly. 'Do you think she's right?' he asked us.

'Course,' said Will.

'And what do you say, Bess?'

'I think . . .' I said, 'I think somehow we were meant to come here.' And Little Jim seemed happy with the idea. He waved his soggy biscuit in the air and kicked his legs in delight.

'Well, who am I to argue, then?' said Father. 'Of course there'll be things I've got to look into first. So I'm not making any promises, but all being well I don't see why we shouldn't be moved in by Christmas.'

A few miles later, after we'd all been quiet with our own thoughts, Father said suddenly, 'You know the nicest thing about it all?'

'What dear?' said Mother.

'Do you know who lived in that place years ago?' Mother shook her head. 'Sir Walter Raleigh,' said Father.

'Walter Raleigh?' said Mother. 'Isn't he an ancestor of yours? I remember Gran said something about it once.'

'Think so,' said Father. 'Strange how his name keeps cropping up.' I could see him thinking about it, but he said no more.

'Then we'll be buying a place that belonged to your family hundreds of years ago, won't we?' said Mother. 'I think that's wonderful. It's like Bess said, perhaps it was meant. Good thing I bumped into that old man outside the church. I wonder who on earth he was. Tell you one thing, I hope I bump into him again. We've got a lot to thank him for.'

More than you know, I thought. More than you'll ever know.

When we got back to Aunty Ellie's we found a black car parked outside and a tall, grey-suited man waiting for us in the sitting room. Aunty Ellie introduced him and said he was the Lord Lieutenant of the county, whatever that meant. From the way he stood and from the shine on his shoes he looked extremely important, you could tell that much. And what he had to say made even Humph sit up and listen.

'I am commanded by Her Majesty the Queen to accompany you all tomorrow to London, to Buckingham Palace, for a private audience with Her Majesty. Her Majesty wishes to convey to you personally her thanks for your help in recovering the golden orb, and she will, I believe, personally present you with your reward.'

'What, me as well?' said Gran, sitting down before she fell down.

'Everyone, including the dog I believe,' said the Lord Lieutenant looking at Humph with great respect. 'Particularly the dog.'

Well, of course, we couldn't sleep much that night. Will and I were sharing a room at Aunty Ellie's and we lay in the dark and talked and talked about Hayes Barton, about the Queen, about our friend Walter and his amazing master plan. 'I just wish I could see him again,' I said. 'Just once.'

'In truth,' said a voice from the direction of the chest of drawers, 'you have been patient long enough, dear cousins both.' His voice, no doubt of it. I sat up and switched on the bedside light. Walter was standing in between the beds looking down on us. 'So,' he said, sitting down on my bed. 'All is well that ends well, and it has ended well for all of us.

You have your farm and I will have my family back in Hayes Barton where they belong. We have taken back what was mine, what was rightly ours.'

'It was you all along wasn't it?' I said. 'You sent out the invitations for that party to everyone, didn't you?'

He smiled and took my hand. 'To begin with chick, it was mere curiosity. I wished to see my descendants, to see what had become of them all. You can understand that, can you not?'

'But why me?' I asked. 'At the party, why did you come and talk to me?'

'Ah, sweet cousin,' he said, patting my hand. 'There fate indeed took a hand as she does in all things. It was you that found me, for I was sitting surveying my descendants when you came and sat beside me. And then it was that I saw your name – you had it writ upon you if you remember – Bess Throckmorton – as you know, the very name of my dear, dear wife whom I saw at once that you resembled in more than name. 'Twas fate, cousin Bess, that brought us together and led us into this merry dance. I asked you to free me from my prison and take me home to Devon with you, and you did. So I learned of your father's misfortune and began to conceive my plan. But alas, my schemes all miscarried when your grandmother became ill.'

'But one thing I've never understood,' I said. 'Why did you take Sally away like that and where did you go?'

'How else was I to get to Hayes Barton and play the ghost?

I had to make the farm available, did I not? I knew of only one certain way to do it.'

'You became headless, didn't you?' said Will. 'And you frightened them off, like you did with the horrible Barrowbills. Brilliant! Wicked!'

'Wicked it may be but it never fails, it seems,' said Sir Walter. 'Let us say that I persuaded them they would be happier somewhere else.'

'That was a bit cruel,' I said.

'Sometimes you have to be cruel to be kind, cousin,' said Walter.

'You're beginning to sound like Gran,' I said.

'What about the reward, though?' Will asked – he was asking all the questions I wanted to ask. 'How did you know there would be a reward?'

'I confess,' said Walter, 'I confess that fortune favoured us in this, but fortune once stirred can act most powerfully in our endeavours. If truth be told it was on impulse that I took the bauble and I was at my wit's end to know what to do with it. I saw you that night secreting it in the muck heap. So I dug it up myself, for I needed time to consider what might be done with it.'

'And the search up at the horrible Barrowbills' was just a game, wasn't it?' I said.

'Indeed,' said Walter smiling, 'but one I think we all enjoyed.'

'We're going to see the Queen tomorrow,' I said.

'I know it, cousin,' said Walter.

'You didn't arrange that as well, did you?' Will said.

'Faith, no,' Walter laughed.

'Why don't you come with us?' I asked.

He shook his head. 'I have had my fill of kings and queens,' he said. 'I will wait for you at Hayes Barton.'

'You'll be there?' I asked. He nodded.

'If you do not mind, cousin,' he said.

'That's what you really wanted all along, wasn't it?' said Will. 'You wanted to come back and live at Hayes Barton.'

'I perceive you are as sharp as I am, Master Will, a chip off the old block some might say, though that's not a phrase I care for overmuch.' And he rubbed the back of his neck. 'Yes indeed, look for me at Hayes. I shall be there.' And he was gone.

Buckingham Palace was all crunchy gravel and long corridors and pictures as big as houses. Father looked a bit stiff, I thought – he always looked uncomfortable in a suit – and when it came to it he got his bow all wrong. But Mother looked as if she belonged there. She had her best dress on – the kingfisher blue one with the gold braid. She curtsied beautifully and was soon chatting away to the Queen as if they were old friends. Little Jim was wide-eyed throughout. He sucked his hand all the time and dribbled. And Will and me? Well, we were so terrified that we could hardly say a word.

Gran and Aunty Ellie smiled perpetually and kept licking their lips frantically in case they cracked. Humph was just himself. We had him on a lead, (a brand new one, of course), just in case the corgies were around. There's not a lot of difference in size between a big rabbit and a corgi and I didn't want him disgracing himself.

So we came home after our great day in London. Father bought Hayes Barton and we moved in before Christmas. My friend Walter comes and goes as he pleases. Of course he only appears to Will and me, and he never goes headless anywhere. We insisted on that. So I suppose you could say he really has become one of the family.

On Christmas Day we were out walking together, my friend Walter and me, when I dared at last to ask him what I'd always longed to ask him. 'All right,' he said. 'I'll do it just this once, and only for you.'

And at that he took his cloak off and with a grand flourish laid it down across a muddy gateway. I held his hand and tiptoed across it in my wellingtons. 'Thy servant, Your Majesty,' he said.

'Thou art indeed a true friend,' I said in my queenliest voice. 'And I would have thee by my side forever.'

'So you will, my lady,' he said bowing low. 'So you will.'